ADVANCE PRAISE FOR
Same Time Next Summer

"Annabel Monaghan's *Same Time Next Summer* is an unforgettable love story. Packed with longing and bursting with the magic of first love, it's everything I want in a summer romance. I devoured it!"

—Carley Fortune, author of *Every Summer After*

"Is there anything better than an oceanfront novel about the enduring power of summer love? Annabel Monaghan's witty, wild *Same Time Next Summer* has it all: beachfront parties, complex characters, and hearts that won't be silenced. I loved this fun, heartfelt book."

—Amanda Eyre Ward, author of *The Jetsetters* and *The Lifeguards*

"Annabel Monaghan secures her spot on my auto-buy authors list with this gorgeous second-chance romance. *Same Time Next Summer* absolutely captured my heart from the very beginning, and I couldn't help rooting for these characters to find their happily ever after. This book is the definition of a perfect beach read and should be on everyone's summer reading list!"

—Falon Ballard, author of *Lease on Love* and *Just My Type*

"Hands down, my favorite book of the summer. It was beautifully written, full of delightful characters, and kept me feeling nostalgic for that fizzy, all-consuming intensity of first love. I absolutely adored it!"

—Lacie Waldon, author of *The Layover* and *From the Jump*

"Deftly weaving past and present into a gorgeously rendered tale of love, self-discovery, and the experiences—and people—that define our lives, Monaghan's *Same Time Next Summer* wrapped me in a nostalgic blanket of heart-melting romance warmer than a beachside vacation. This is second-chance romance at its absolute finest . . . a story you do *not* want to miss!"

—Angie Hockman, author of *Dream On* and *Shipped*

"Elegant and richly emotional, *Same Time Next Summer* offers a romantic story of the renewing joy of second chances. We never wanted to leave the summer shores and gorgeous pages of this lyrical love story."

—Emily Wibberley and Austin Siegemund-Broka, authors of *The Roughest Draft*

"*Same Time Next Summer* is a second-chance romance infused with beach sand, sunsets, and finding your heart's one true love. Monaghan crafts a compulsively readable tale about falling in love, not just with the person of your heart, but also with yourself and the you that you were always destined to be. Witty and wonderful, this book should be on the top of everyone's to-be-read pile!"

—Jenn McKinlay, author of *Wait For It*

"Delicious, like a bag of chips you can't put down until it's finished. I loved it!"
—Jane L. Rosen, author of *Nine Women, One Dress* and *Eliza Starts a Rumor*

"Annabel Monaghan has done it again with impossible-not-to-love characters that stumble off the page in all their messy glory. This effervescent novel is perfect for anyone who's ever wished they could bottle up the magic of their first summer romance—and uncork it decades later."
—Christina Clancy, author of *The Second Home* and *Shoulder Season*

"*Same Time Next Summer* is just the swoony romance we all want and need! With characters who feel like family and a picture-perfect beach setting, Monaghan has written a beautiful love story, full of wit, wisdom, and heart."
—Amy Poeppel, author of *Musical Chairs*

"Annabel Monaghan has worked her alchemy again: With heart, humor, and the trademark wit that gives her writing a sophisticated zing, she's spun an irresistibly evocative tale of young love lost and, after some understandable but unfortunate missteps, deliciously found. Take this one to the beach, but be forewarned: you'll be so swept away by thirty-year-old Sam, newly engaged and craving stability, and her first love, Wyatt, that you might not notice the tide coming in."
—Karen Dukess, author of *The Last Book Party*

"Every word of *Same Time Next Summer* draws you in, affecting on a deep, emotional level. Prepare for a journey through unforgettable first love, its marriage to music, and the wit and charm that make Monaghan's books fresh and original. Sam and Wyatt are the fated lovers readers will root for over and over again, a tale rich and heartfelt. This is the love story of 2023."

—Rochelle Weinstein, author of *When We Let Go*

PRAISE FOR

Nora Goes Off Script

One of *Cosmopolitan*'s 30 Best Romance Novels of 2022
That'll Give You All the Feels

One of *Southern Living*'s Beach Reads
Perfect for Summer 2022

One of *theSkimm*'s 10 Books
That'll Get You Out of a Reading Rut

"A witty and poignant roller coaster that springs a delightful surprise." —*People*

"Monaghan's witty adult debut novel perfectly captures the apprehension and excitement of infatuation blended with life's complications." —*The Washington Post*

Same
Time
Next
Summer

ALSO BY ANNABEL MONAGHAN

Nora Goes Off Script

Same Time Next Summer

Annabel Monaghan

G. P. PUTNAM'S SONS

New York

PUTNAM
— EST. 1838 —

G. P. PUTNAM'S SONS

Publishers Since 1838

An imprint of Penguin Random House LLC

penguinrandomhouse.com

Library of Congress Cataloging-in-Publication Data

Names: Monaghan, Annabel, author.
Title: Same time next summer / Annabel Monaghan.
Description: New York: G. P. Putnam's Sons, 2023.
Identifiers: LCCN 2023007358 (print) | LCCN 2023007359 (ebook) |
ISBN 9780593544969 (trade paperback) | ISBN 9780593544976 (ebook)
Subjects: LCGFT: Romance fiction. | Novels.
Classification: LCC PS3613.O52268 S36 2023 (print) |
LCC PS3613.O52268 (ebook) | DDC 813/.6—dc23/eng/20230221
LC record available at https://lccn.loc.gov/2023007358
LC ebook record available at https://lccn.loc.gov/2023007359
p.   cm.

Printed in the United States of America
1   3   5   7   9   10   8   6   4   2

Book design by Ashley Tucker
Interior art © Shutterstock/AlinArt

For Stefanie

Same
Time
Next
Summer

PART 1

NOW & THEN

NOW

1

You can't turn around once you're in the tunnel. There's no U-turn, no off-ramp. You're literally stuck under the East River. This fact exhilarated me as a kid. *Next stop, Long Island.* At the first sight of sunlight at the end of the tunnel, I felt the city melt away. I cracked the window, popped a juice box, kicked off my shoes, and stretched my legs across the backseat. As an adult, entering the Midtown Tunnel makes me feel sort of trapped.

The traffic slows to a standstill as we merge onto the Long Island Expressway. "And this is why we don't come to Long Island," I say, swatting the steering wheel like it's responsible. I'm not sure what I was expecting on a Friday afternoon in August.

"We both know that's not why," says Jack, scrolling through his phone.

I can handle Long Island once a summer for a long weekend, never a week. Three days at the beach is enough to warm you up but not enough to turn you into mush. For three days in a row, my sister, Gracie, drags me into the ocean, and for three days in a row, I swim. I count my strokes as I cut through the water and long for the constraints of the YMCA pool, where you can track how far you've gone based on how many times you've turned around. The ocean is a full mile long on the stretch of beach between the jetty and the wooded cove in front of our house. There's just too much room for error.

It's been fourteen years since I've spent a whole summer at the beach—since Wyatt and I broke up, and I broke apart. Putting a person back together isn't easy, but if you're smart about it you can reassemble yourself in a totally different, better way. Turn carefree into careful; bandage up your heart and double-check the adhesive. Bit by bit, I have left my childhood behind, replacing my impulsiveness with deliberate decisions and plans. Jack calls it being buttoned up, and I don't know why anyone would want to walk around unbuttoned. I know what each day is going to look like even before I open my eyes, and there's so much strength in that knowing. If I stay at the beach for too long, I get pulled back. My old self is there and she wants to drag me out through the rusty chinks in my armor. I blame the salt air.

This is the first time I've brought Jack with me in the entire four years we've been together. Travis likes to say that I've been protecting him from our parents, which is ridiculous because we see them in Manhattan all the time. Part of me has wanted to show Jack the front-yard hydrangea explosion and the delicate way the dunes blow in parallel to the ocean. To show him where the sand and the salt and the sun conspired to make me into a strong swimmer and a happy teenager. I just don't know if he can handle the summer version of my parents.

Traffic picks up when we're on Sunrise Highway, and Jack puts down his phone. "It's pretty here," he says as if looking out the window for the first time. "I found a gym ten minutes from your parents' house and got a week's membership."

"There's no way we're staying a whole week." I've packed exactly three pairs of underwear to make sure of it.

"Well you told your mom a week. Anyway, I took next week off, just in case. It's going to be a hundred degrees in the city by Thursday." He takes my hand, and I feel myself settle. Jack is the opposite of the ocean. He's more like a lake, one that's crystal clear and protected by a mountain range. With Jack, I am in no danger of being washed away. "This might be really fun."

He's scrolling through his phone again. "Oh, here's a good one. A listing for an in-house HR associate at an accounting firm in midtown."

"They're not going to fire me," I say. They're probably going to fire me. I'm in the firing business, and I can't imagine how this ends any other way. Frankly, I'd fire me, but I'm so sick of talking about this and the tight, defensive way it makes my body feel.

"They might, Sam." He puts his hand on my shoulder. "Eleanor's way of doing things is tried and true."

"I said what I said, and I apologized. It's out of my hands."

"If you're going to go off the rails, you kind of need a backup plan," Jack says.

"I'll remember that for next time. So are you ready for what you're walking into? Hippies gone wild?" My smile is a question mark. "There's no Wi-Fi or air-conditioning, but if you're looking to see a statue of David made out of pipe cleaners, this is the place for you."

Jack laughs, presumably because he thinks I'm exaggerating. "I've been wanting to see this for years, I'm ready as hell."

Jack knows my parents in the city, between the months of September and May, where they live in the same Lower East Side two-bedroom, rent-controlled apartment that Travis and I and then Gracie grew up in. After thirty-two years in that apartment, they practically live for free. My dad teaches art history at NYU, and my mom teaches modern poetry at the New School. They are like squirrels in reverse—from September to May they toil and save so that they can spend the summer at the beach doing whatever they want. Jack likes the school-year version of my parents. He thinks they seem like people in a Woody Allen movie, real New Yorkers.

In October we'll be married. Jack's parents have put down a small deposit for an October 28 wedding at their country club in Connecticut, but we haven't fully committed. The venue is beautiful and easy—they literally have three wedding options: A, B, and C. They all seem pretty much the same to me, but Jack likes B. I wanted to get married on the lawn outside the boathouse in Central Park underneath the beech trees, but apparently that gets booked up years in advance, which I find fascinating, like brides are booking venues before they've even met the guy. I don't know how I missed this.

We were ready to press go on Jack's B wedding when my mom put her foot down. She loves Jack and is definitely relieved to see me so happy, but as the wedding gets closer she's starting to feel left out of the planning. She feels like the spirit of my family isn't being represented. When she called to lay this on me, I held my ground.

"Please come have a look at the Old Sloop Inn out here. Come get reacquainted with this place and yourself. Show Jack who we are." I said no.

But when Gracie asked me to come, I caved. Unless it's been something directly related to her safety, I don't think I've ever said no to Gracie. "Please come, Sammy," she'd said. "Just so Mom feels better. Jack will love it. It'll be perfect."

As far as Jack's concerned, things have been pretty perfect. We met getting into opposite sides of a cab and then shared a ride to where I was visiting a client two blocks from his dermatology practice (perfect). It happened to be right after I'd gotten a haircut and a blowout, so I looked like the most aspirational version of myself (perfect). A year later we moved into an apartment over our favorite sushi place (perfect). He proposed to me with a one-carat solitaire diamond ring that belonged to his grandmother, who happened to also have a size six ring finger (perfect).

When we're finally off the highway, Jack puts down his window and takes a showy whiff of the salt air. Jack bought this convertible BMW in a moment of madness I can't quite put a context to, though he's never once taken the top off on account of the sun. Every time I get in, I wonder if his alter ego appeared one day and bought it, a Bizarro World version

of Superman, one who welcomes sun on his face and toler-
ates unkempt hair. It both delights and terrifies me to think
that he could also go totally off the rails for a minute.

I turn left onto West Main Street, past the Episcopal
church, the deli, Chippy's Diner, and the library. I haven't
been to Oak Shore since last summer when Jack went on a
golf trip with his brothers. I have the sensation that the
town is going to notice a disturbance in the force. *Hey, Sam,
who's the new guy? Well done.*

I finally turn right toward the beach and onto Saltaire
Lane. We pass Wyatt's house, a stately brick thing with
black shutters to match the high-gloss front door. There's a
light on in the front room. I haven't been inside the Popes'
house since the summer I was sixteen, but I could walk into
that house blindfolded and get myself a glass of water. They
rent it to strangers now.

There's a tall hedge between Wyatt's house and ours. I
slow down to take it in. It's technically on the property line,
so both of our families are responsible for maintaining it.
Wyatt's dad, Frank, always wanted to hire someone to deal
with it and split the cost, but my dad wouldn't have it. The
hedge, or "privet" as he calls it, using air quotes, is an honor
to maintain. He trims it with small clippers and no measur-
ing stick. Some years it's wavy on top, some years it reaches
a high peak in the middle. It's never, ever straight, and this
year it leans toward the ocean.

The beach house and every tree and bush on the property are a great source of pride to my dad. He bought the
house and eventually paid off the mortgage during a decade
when he had epic success as an abstract artist. It started with

a painting called *Current*, which is basically swirls of black and white on a sky-blue background. Galleries all over the country sold versions of this painting as quickly as he could produce them. I was just a kid, but I loved seeing him emerge from his studio with canvas after canvas. I thought it would go on forever. But when the zeitgeist changed and the demand for swirly dried up, he was never able to come up with the next thing. He's now fifteen years into a dry spell, and this property is what he has left.

To my eye, the hedge is approximately the eight feet tall that it's always been, but it seems denser from years of branches comingling. Throughout my childhood, Frank thanked my dad for doing the hedges with a nice bottle of scotch at the end of the summer. I assume the scotch stopped coming after Marion and Frank divorced. The real barrier between our houses is now as much psychic as physical anyway.

"Are we here?" Jack asks.

"No, that next one."

The sound of tires on gravel welcomes us into our driveway. People say it's hard to tell if our house is a house with a porch or a porch with a house. The porch wraps around the entire ground floor and is comparable in square footage. Wisteria lines the railing, climbing up the posts and running along the gutters like delicately placed lavender frosting. The smell of the wisteria welcomes you in from the street and then lures you around corners to the ocean view.

Jack's already gotten out of the car, and I take a deep breath. I look out over the steering wheel and feel like I'm about to watch a home movie. I'm not sure I want to press play, but I get out of the car anyway. Gracie barrels out the front door, all limbs and dark braids waving in the air. "Sammy!" she calls, racing past Jack to get to me. I bury my nose in the top of her head and am transported back to when the weight of her infant body in my arms felt like the only thing that was keeping me alive. The sweet smell of her hair and the fierce energy of her hug have kept me tethered to the earth for a long time. My twelve-year-old sister is a walking, singing, laughing silver lining.

"Hey, kiddo," I say. "Did you say hi to Jack?" This is rhetorical, as we both know she did not.

"Hi." She gives a quick wave.

"You want to fill us in on what we're walking into?"

"Granny and Gramps are here. They seem older than at Christmas. Travis and Hugh are coming for dinner. There's lots of talk about where you two are sleeping, like before you're married." Gracie blushes and I try to remember what it was like to be twelve.

"Eew," I say. "In the same room with him?"

"Right? So gross. So I think he's staying in the garage apartment."

Jack doesn't seem to mind. "Water view?"

Gracie gives him a *yikes* face. "Looks over where we keep the garbage cans. And the garage is where Dad paints so it kind of smells like poison."

"Is he painting?" I ask.

"I don't think so. Last week I could smell paint, but he was just opening cans. All his brushes are clean."

"Well, it sounds like a good spot for me. My own bachelor pad," Jack says.

"Sam, sweetheart!" It's my mom. She's in a lavender caftan to match the wisteria, her dark hair swept back off her face as if she got out of the ocean and just let it dry like that. No makeup, no shoes. She's painted her toenails silver.

I give her a hug. "Hi, Mom."

She beams. "Jack! Welcome. We're thrilled you're finally here." She takes his face in her hands as she says this, and I see him wince. Jack has a thing about foreign oils (on my mom I'm guessing Coppertone and canola) mixing with his Serum Hydrée.

"Hello, Laurel," he says, and kisses her cheek.

Gracie locks her arm in mine and leads me up the stairs to the porch. "Mom put flowers in your room and changed your sheets twice." I feel briefly guilty that I haven't been here all summer.

When I have the door halfway open, the smell surrounds me. Old Bay seasoning, sourdough bread. And something fishy I can't identify. This is what summer smelled like.

Jack steps in beside me. "It's a lot of stuff," he says.

I look around. It is, truly, a lot of stuff. This is how our beach house has always looked, sort of like a preschool classroom before they sing the cleanup song. A low table in the entry hall is covered in mason jars filled with shells, sea glass, and self-adhesive googly eyes. A large jar overflows with seaweed, which explains the fishy smell. My dad collects seaweed to use as paintbrushes, which I'm not ready to explain to Jack.

Right past that collection is a wide hallway where the

dining room table has been shoved against the wall. On it are piles of sticks and larger pieces of driftwood. There are vats of water and a drying rack. This is my mom's pet project, making a single sheet of paper and then printing the first copy of a new poem on it. She says it's a ritual of gratitude. I can't even describe what a mess it is to make paper.

"What's all this?" Jack says, almost to himself. It alarms me to see our house through his eyes. Their apartment in the city is packed with papers and books, but it's small and efficient in a way that Jack appreciates. This place, with its endless collections of what he must consider garbage, is a whole other story.

"Makes her own paper," is all I can get out.

"Sam!" My dad comes in from the back porch, letting the screen door snap behind him. He's tan and his silver hair almost touches his shoulders. He looks like an ad for expensive beer. "Well if it isn't Sam Holloway's annual visit to the beach! Nothing makes me happier than seeing you out here." I give him a one-armed hug. There was a time when I would run up to my dad and hug him so fiercely that my feet would lift right off the ground. I love my dad, but I don't worship him anymore. As I've gotten older, I've learned that it's totally possible to love someone from a safe distance.

"Bill. You have a beautiful home," Jack says with as much conviction as he can muster.

"Thanks. We've got a lot going on, that's for sure. Now come out back. We have a slew of old people with serious opinions about how close you should be sleeping to my daughter."

MY GRANDPARENTS ARE the best, hands down. They're straightforward and familiar and not at all afraid to tell you what's up. When they came from Pennsylvania to visit us the first Christmas after Jack and I moved in together, Granny was quick to criticize our muted, minimalist apartment: "I've seen prisons with more personality." My parents gasped, and Granny and Gramps laughed and laughed. That's how it is with both of them, machine-gun fire of thoughts and opinions and then a big laugh that tells you none of it mattered at all.

We find them on the porch, and they cry out, "The bride!" in unison. Someone has given Granny a kazoo, and she blows it.

My mom pours mai tais, which seem out of place but, I admit, are delicious. Each one is adorned with a handmade cocktail umbrella, found sticks glued to scraps of homemade paper. Jack immediately plucks his out and checks his glass for debris. I don't know how to tell him that there's a little bit of sand in everything at the beach. Also, glue.

There's a toast and a lot of small talk, and I take in the welcome beauty of the Atlantic Ocean. Just beyond the porch, the thick run of dunes leads to a stretch of beach that leads to the shore. The sun is low and casts speckled light on the water. The gulls soar and dive as the waves roll in, one after another, reaching out and pulling back in an infinite loop. The endlessness of it all overwhelms me. I feel like the ocean should have stopped and changed when I did.

"Your boyfriend is here," Granny is saying.

"Mother!" my mom scolds, and looks at me. The words

register first in my chest, which is suddenly tight and hot. She can't mean Wyatt.

Gracie sits up straight.

Granny smiles over her nearly empty mai tai. "Oh, you know what I mean. Your old flame, Wyatt." Then to Jack, "She lost her mind over that one."

I am staring at a spot on the table, just beyond my hands, where my mom has placed a citronella candle in the shape of a conch shell. I'm afraid the heat from my chest and the panic in my eyes might melt it into a puddle of wax. "What do you mean 'here'?" I ask without looking up. "Like on the East Coast? Or at the house?"

My mother briefly looks guilty. "Well, I meant to tell you. Right there at the house. I guess Marion didn't rent it this summer, because he's been there for a while." She stirs the pitcher of mai tais and refills Jack's glass.

"You know Wyatt?" Gracie asks me. Gracie's asking me about Wyatt, and it throws me like a wave after a hurricane. Everyone is looking at me for a response. There is a loud ringing in my ears and the heat in my chest has spread to my face. Jack knows the story. And he knows how incendiary all of this is.

"Well, I've heard all about Wyatt," Jack says. "The whole reason I became a doctor was so that I could compete with a guy with a guitar." Nervous laughter titters over empty mai tais.

"I see him all the time," says Gracie. "He lets me watch him surf. And he's teaching me to play 'Leaving on a Jet Plane' on the guitar. He has a bunch of guitars up there."

"Up where?" asks Jack.

"In the treehouse," says Gracie. This makes Jack laugh, and I try to make sense of it. There is not one funny thing about that treehouse. Or Wyatt. Or the fact that I'm thirty years old and feeling panicked about seeing the guy who broke my heart when I was a teenager.

Wyatt's dad helped his brother, Michael, and him build that treehouse in the oak tree between their pool and the dunes when they were ten and twelve years old, spending days at junkyards and shipyards all over Long Island. While I can remember falling in love in small moments all over the beach and while floating on the ocean, I lost my virginity specifically in that treehouse. At night, after my house went quiet, I would sneak downstairs and out the back door and through the dunes to the rope ladder that led to Wyatt. He'd say, "Hey, Sam-I-am," and he'd kiss me, and I'd wonder if there were any two people in the world who were more right together.

The treehouse would last forever, Wyatt once told me, because there were no walls in the front or back. A storm would blow right through it. The tree itself grew to form a bit of a back wall, giving us privacy in case Marion and Frank happened to be peering out their bedroom window with binoculars. But the front was wide open to the ocean view, Wyatt's beach chair next to mine. Eventually, just a jumble of bodies and blankets.

My chest is still tight, and I cannot wrestle my face into neutral. I study my drink and use my handmade umbrella to try to fish a tiny piece of pineapple out of my mai tai. I haven't seen Wyatt since I was sixteen, haven't spoken to him since I was eighteen. It was teenage infatuation, and

Dr. Judy even went so far as to call it addiction, but it's been a long time and I'm a rebuilt grown-up person with a real live fiancé and a career. I recently contributed to a 401(k), for God's sake. I can't imagine seeing Wyatt now, introducing him to Jack and asking about life in Los Angeles. *So hey, how'd that all work out?* Wyatt is a locked-away memory of a time I don't want to go back to and a person I can barely remember being. And somehow he's thirty feet away, right next door. I'm not sure I would have come if they'd told me he was here. Which probably explains why they didn't tell me.

"You know Wyatt," I say to Gracie. Just to confirm. Just to nail down one single fact that will keep everything I know from blowing away with the next breeze off the ocean.

"Yep," she says. "He knew who I was right away."

TRAVIS AND HUGH are late for dinner, but we've all had enough mai tais and cashews not to care. "Nice slacks," is the first thing Travis says to me. I haven't seen him since Easter, when he commented that I was dressed like a Delta flight attendant.

I hug Hugh before I say, "They're called chinos in the catalog. I think they're even called 'favorite chinos.' They're what people who don't surf all day wear."

"Ah, I didn't know they made catalogs just for tax accountants," Travis says.

"Cute. How far did you have to chase the Hawaiian Punch guy to get that shirt?" I ask, and toss another cashew into my mouth. This is our love language, but Jack thinks Travis is threatened by how much I've made of my career when all he does is surf and pick out fabrics all day. Jack's being overly loyal, because Travis and Hugh actually do really well. They have a booming architecture and design business in town, Travis being the aesthetic director and Hugh being the actual architect. My parents have expected their engagement for longer than they'd been expecting mine.

My dad barbecues sausages, and my mom's made a salad and scalloped potatoes. We eat at the long table on the back porch, as usual, as the sun puts on a dramatic show of setting. I can do this for three days. As long as I can avoid Wyatt. He's not going to just walk up onto our deck, and I could put Gracie on lookout and let her run interference for me. I take in my immediate family, my grandparents, and my handsome fiancé. We've sat like this dozens of times since Jack and I met, mostly in my parents' cramped dining room in the city. But it's different here, like a step back in time to who my family used to be.

"So have they started selling you on the Old Sloop Inn yet?" Hugh asks. "The garden can accommodate two hundred people and the food's great."

"That's what we're here for. To check out all our options," Jack says, and gives my hand a squeeze. My mom smiles at the sight of our hands together.

"I think you're going to love it. And it has thirty guest rooms for out-of-towners," says my mom. And then, "Of course your parents would be welcome to stay here," which stops my heart. Jack's mom does not make her own paper. In fact, her paper comes in a lovely box with her initials printed in navy blue in the upper left-hand corner. Like a normal person.

Travis shakes his head. "I think it's unbelievable that you haven't nailed this down yet. I figured you would have laid all this out in a spreadsheet the day you got engaged."

I shrug. It is planned, of course. Jack picked B. It's not the beach wedding I imagined as a kid or the Central Park wedding I imagined the day Jack proposed to me, but it's easy, and I'm sure it will be beautiful.

A few guitar notes come from the treehouse. Everyone's quiet, and I wonder if they can hear my heart beat. I notice I am holding my breath. The same notes come again, then again with a few more added on. He's writing a song in there and I can picture him doing it, his legs dangling over the edge, his brow furrowed. It's like I went out into the world and grew up, and he's still right here. Right where I left him.

2

I wake in my childhood bedroom to the early morning light coming through the window and briefly don't know where I am. The sound of the waves crashing outside isn't so different from the rush of cars down Lexington Avenue. My double bed is pushed up against the pale yellow wall on which is painted my terrible version of the tree of life. I got the idea for this project the summer that Wyatt and Michael were building their treehouse. I wanted one of my own, but there was no tree for it on our property, so I decided I would turn my bedroom into a treehouse by painting a gigantic tree on the wall. My dad was working in his studio when I asked him for a can of brown paint. He pointed to a stack of cans in the corner, not looking up from his work. We were all artists then, no questions asked.

I spent a week working on it and wouldn't let any of the boys in my room until I was done. Wyatt was the only one who wanted to see it anyway. Looking at the big brown trunk and its leafless branches now, I understand fully why I don't like working with paint. Paint drips and bleeds and responds to gravity. Of course this is why my dad loves it; he's practically reckless. At the time, he was thrilled with my wall, probably by the effort more than the outcome. He put his arm around me as he ran his eyes over every branch. "I love it," he said. "Needs texture."

I check my phone and it's only six. I lie back down and pull the covers up over my head to see if I can go back to sleep, and also to avoid taking in the rest of the time capsule that sits on my open rolltop desk. A jar full of sea glass. Three swimming trophies. A red ribbon from the Summer Muffin-a-thon. Stacks of self-indulgent journals that I decide I will throw out today.

In the drawer of the desk is a sketch pad that contains early versions of the drawing I did of Wyatt. I don't need to take it out; I see them perfectly in my mind. It was a super-alive summer, when all of my senses were on a delicious high alert. It was the summer I noticed everything—the way the salt dried on my skin, the way sand settled between my toes. The way Wyatt smiled at me while he was composing a song. We hung the final version of my drawing on a rusty nail on the treehouse wall, back before we knew how easily precious things could disintegrate in the salt air.

As I get out of bed, I think about how memories are just fine the way nature made them. We are forward-moving people, so as we go through life our unnecessary memories fade until we finally shed them. The ones we need—the time you touched the hot oven, the time you slipped on black ice—those memories burrow into our psyches to keep us safe. But there's no reason to walk into the museum of your childhood just for old times' sake. It's confusing to be faced with all the things you used to think were important once you've grown up. If I were my parents, I would have changed this room into a gym.

I find Gramps on the back porch, waiting for someone to make him coffee. "Oh, thank God," he says when he sees me. "You know Annie's going to sleep till ten and I don't know how the hell that contraption in there works."

I brew the coffee and make raisin toast, buttered and with marmalade, the way he likes it. I head back out and place the tray on the table between our chairs.

"Ah, lovely," he says. "What a wife you'll be."

"Gramps."

"Antiquated?"

"Definitely." I sip my coffee and notice it tastes different here. There's something about the beach that changes the chemical components of everything around it. Wood feels damp, sheets right out of the dryer still smell of salt. And the coffee, it's just better.

"Sounds to me like you're making your own money now anyway. Maybe he should be making you breakfast." He gives me a sideways glance to let me know he's just trying to get me going.

"I do make plenty of money, Gramps."

"Good for you," he says. "Cracks me up that people pay you to boss them around."

"It's not bossing them around so much as setting standards," I say. "We take a fact-based approach to human capital and create measurable outcomes."

"Sounds like nonsense," he says, and I guess it does. I say that sentence so often I don't even hear it anymore. I've been working for Eleanor Schultz for eight years and her approach to human resources consulting is like her religion, and mine too. The beauty is that there's never any kind of misunderstanding between people; you never have to wonder. If we tell you that you need to score eight on some scale and you score seven, you're fired. We can literally point to the chart that made the decision, so no hard feelings.

I met Eleanor during my senior year at NYU at a recruiting event. She was wearing her signature black wool suit and seemed completely in control of herself and her surroundings, even as she sat at a folding table in a hard metal chair. The banner behind her said HUMAN CORPS: PRODUCTIVE PEOPLE, PREDICTABLE OUTCOMES. And I just loved that. I wanted to wrap myself in that banner and enjoy a lifetime of predictable outcomes. No more surprises, no more broken promises. Just people doing what they say they're going to do. Eleanor may have mistaken my enthusiasm for the concept with enthusiasm for the job, but a few weeks later, I was hired.

"The thing I like about Human Corps is that we help people succeed by making rules that they can live by. Then they just get to decide if they want to do what it takes to keep their jobs."

"Human Core? Like an apple?"

"No, like 'Peace Corps.'"

"So if you write it down it looks like 'human corpse'?" Gramps laughs. He puts down his coffee and says it again, "Human corpse." Soon he is laughing so hard that he has to take off his glasses to wipe his eyes. He takes a giant handkerchief out of his pocket and blows his nose.

His laughing makes me smile, and I don't remember the last time my body gave itself over to a laugh that way. Human Corpse. I'll never be able to unsee that.

"Kind of a lifeless job you've got there, sweetie," he says, still laughing.

"It can be rigid," I say.

"A bunch of stiffs in suits." He's wiping his eyes again.

It baffles me that I ever did anything to compromise this job. I like the people, I like the processes, and I like how I know exactly how things are going to turn out. It's the perfect job for me. My mistake was suggesting something new to a client. Looking back now, I see it was ridiculous. When Eleanor called me into her office, she blamed my engagement. According to her, in the past year I've been less predictable, which is a pretty big insult coming from her. It's been a week since this all went down, and it feels like temporary insanity more than anything else.

Granny appears on the porch, in a nightgown and a cardigan sweater. "You two had better thank God you made enough coffee for me. It sounds like there's a hyena out here." She takes a long sip from her mug and looks out at the water. "What's so funny anyway?"

"Sam's a human corpse," says Gramps, blowing his nose again.

Granny turns toward the water. She's focused on a very specific spot. "Is that a dolphin or a person?"

While Granny sees pretty well for eighty-four, you wouldn't exactly trust her to land a plane. I get up to have a look. The water is calm. It's a paddleboarder moving parallel to the horizon, a big hat on his head. And I know. I can tell from the way he moves. Even though the Wyatt I knew didn't paddleboard. I don't even think that was a thing back then.

My heart rate quickens and my breath gets shallow as we stare. My memory fills in his features, his wide-set brown eyes. The way his hair curled up on the left side of his widow's peak. The furrow of his brow. I wonder if he'd be doing that now, concentrating on the water.

"It's him," I say almost to myself, but of course to Granny because I need her help. "He feels like a ghost."

Granny puts her arm around me. "And I bet he's still holding a candle for you too."

"Oh for God's sake," I say, wiggling out of her embrace. "No one's holding a candle for anyone. That was over a decade ago, we were kids."

"Oh my," Gramps says. "Strong feelings."

The two of them. Honestly the cutest people I've ever wanted to strangle. "Okay, enough. We're going to pretend he's not here and focus all of our energy on the man I'm actually marrying. The good one. The doctor."

JACK SLEEPS UNTIL nine, which surprises me. He's normally up and at the gym by seven, but the garage apartment is dark and he slept right through. Jack works out four (never five) days a week in our building gym, alternating between push day, pull day, and leg day. On the other days we have Fritz come to our gym with high-intensity workouts that are designed to confuse our muscles into shape. It all feels completely counterintuitive, and sometimes I feel like my muscles are more than confused, but it's an efficient workout and something we do together. Two nights a week, Jack plays tennis with his cardiologist friend Elliot, and Gracie comes over to eat ice cream for dinner.

I'm happy to skip the gym, because it's beautiful on the deck, eighty degrees with the sunlight feathering the water. There's a breeze coming through the dunes that hits me each time my skin starts to feel too warm. The breeze on my skin reminds me of something I don't want to remember. I'm starting to feel the pull of the ocean, and on a day like this, I can't imagine spending ninety minutes in a basement gym confusing my muscles.

I take Jack into town for lunch, and we share a lobster roll and a Caesar salad at Chippy's. We walk down West Main Street afterward, and I point out the ice-cream shop where we used to go in the afternoons and the library where I worked that summer. Oak Shore has known me at every stage of my life—when I was seven and got scolded for running into Ginnie's Bakery without shoes, when I was twelve and rode with the boys in the back of Wyatt's dad's truck in the Fourth of July parade, when I was sixteen and Mrs. Barton called to me at the end of every shift, "Time to go, your Wyatt's outside."

We walk by the Old Sloop Inn, but we don't go in because my mom's going to make us do a deep dive there tomorrow. "Rustic," Jack says. Everyone knows "rustic" is nice for "needs paint."

"Well, yes. It's as old as the town."

"I can't really see you standing in a gown in front of that place."

I look at the inn for a few seconds. "Neither can I. Let's just look at it for my mom, then we can take her to Connecticut, and she'll love it."

"I don't know why I was picturing the Hamptons."

"You're not the first," I say.

Something's off as we meander through town, specifically the fact that no one's meandering. There's a disproportionate number of people who aren't in bathing suits and cover-ups. They're wearing messenger bags and moving quickly.

Jack notices it too. "What's with all the press?"

"Is that who they are?"

"Looks like it. I've seen three guys with camera bags. Think they heard Samantha's back for a wedding venue showdown?"

"Ha."

A smiling older woman approaches, and it takes me a second to recognize Mrs. Barton, our librarian. She drops her grocery bags and pulls me into a hug. "Sam! I can't believe it! I heard you were engaged! Is this him?"

"I'm so happy to see you." I hug her and breathe her in. If it's possible to smell like books, she smells like books. "Yes, this is Jack."

"So handsome! Your mother tells me he's a doctor!" says Mrs. Barton, because maybe she's lost her filter and her command of punctuation.

"It's nice to be back," I say. "We were just noticing all the press, what's that about?"

"So much excitement. There's an amateur music festival

at the Owl Barn this weekend. Lots of up-and-coming musicians are here for it. Usually happens in Newport, but your Wyatt told someone about Oak Shore, and here they are! Great for the local economy, though no one comes to the library." *He's not my Wyatt.*

3

I'm tired when we come back from the commotion of town, and Jack wants to read. Jack and I read a lot. He picks the books, literary fiction mostly, though I have veto power. We read a lot about historical figures, fictionalized to include children and relationships they never had. There are ghosts sometimes, and chapter to chapter, I have a hard time knowing who's talking, but by the time I've finished I feel like I've accomplished something. Sometimes we buy two copies and read the same book at the same time. It's a particular level of intimacy, reading a book with another person. Today we are reading *Wetlands of Westerleigh*, and I'm forty-three pages behind where Jack is. We sit, feet up, on the back porch with our books and iced teas. I pretend to read.

The beach has its own symphony—waves breaking, children playing, gulls squawking. These sounds roll over me, and I remember why I only come back here once a year. Coming home feels like tiptoeing through a minefield, like I could happen upon one particularly compelling shell and all of my hard-earned defenses will be gone. Before yesterday, I couldn't remember the last time I'd thought about Wyatt in more than a passing way. Sometimes I hear that song and think of him, but that can't be helped. As time goes by, it's on the radio less and less, and I steer clear of stations that are playing anything that's not brand-new.

The ocean is reaching out to me and I'm afraid it's going to crack me right open, and there I'll be like a Russian doll, with layers falling off until I'm so small that a seagull could just pluck me out of the sand and swallow me. I remember my body in the ocean, unburdened and strong. I remember the feel of Wyatt's skin on mine for the first time, just where the waves break. I remember standing under the linden tree and willing my hands not to touch his stomach. I haven't thought about that in a long time and the memory of it makes me smile. I close my eyes and remember the kiss that came next. I can feel the breeze off the ocean, I can hear Wyatt's guitar.

"That guy's literally playing the same part over and over. Are we allowed to make requests?" Jack's talking.

I open my eyes and realize it's actually Wyatt's guitar that I'm hearing. "Is that coming from the treehouse?" I ask.

"Sounds like."

I turn to face him. "Do you care that he's here? My old boyfriend? I guess he's here to break into the music business, but I'm sorry it's this weekend."

"Well, it turns up the drama a bit, doesn't it?" Jack laughs a little.

"I know. But you don't mind, do you?" And I realize that I want him to mind. I want Jack to fully understand the seismic impact of that breakup on my life. It's like when you've been covering up an ugly scar but also sort of want to show it to people so they know what you've been through.

"Don't be silly. Why would I care? You were kids." Jack goes back to his book.

THEN

4

Wyatt

The first time Wyatt laid eyes on Sam, she was five years old. He was six and had just finished kindergarten. His family drove up from Florida on the last day of school with his and Michael's feet propped up over coolers in the backseat to find a new family living in what they called the Porch House next door.

Sam was squatting at the base of the maple tree in the front yard, picking up sticks and yelling something at Travis. When Travis saw the car pull up, he immediately disengaged and stood at the edge of the hedge to watch them unload. It was a miracle to show up somewhere and find kids your own age; at least Travis was eight, like Michael. Within the hour, the three boys had climbed the big oak between the pool and the dunes, contemplating but not executing dives from it into the pool. They raced into the ocean and swam until they were forced out by hunger.

Sam's parents met Wyatt's when they came looking for Travis. Bill and Laurel, new in town. Marion and Frank, on their eighth summer in Oak Shore, offering the inside scoop. The adults drank beer and snacked on Fritos and grapes. The boys jumped in and out of the pool, the energy of the third boy revitalizing the games Wyatt and Michael had played for years. Sam sat by her mother, ignored.

WYATT PRETTY MUCH ignored Sam until the summer she was nine. By then, she was a strong swimmer and didn't seem like such a liability. She could hold her own on a boogie board and knew enough not to cry if she got tumbled. They invented a paddle game with lines in the sand that they could all play now that they were a group of four. Wyatt was the first one to call her Sam instead of Samantha, possibly his way of making it okay that he was playing with a girl.

They dug holes and buried themselves in the cool of the undersand. They built sandcastles and carved paths in them for tennis ball races. When these projects deteriorated into the boys' pelting each other with tennis balls as hard as they could, Sam would go home and read in bed or walk down the beach collecting shells. One thing Wyatt always knew about Sam, she knew when she'd had enough.

By the summer that Sam was twelve and Wyatt was thirteen, the foursome was part of a bigger pack of kids. They'd spend the day at the beach, sprawling on an island of towels. Their daily business was swimming and sunbathing. In the afternoon they'd all hop on bikes and head to town for ice cream, biking back to the beach one-handed to carry their cones.

One night in late August (it was almost September, when Sam would have been thirteen, Wyatt liked to remind himself when he thought about this), the kids were on the beach after dinner. The sun was low but not down, that last whisper of a summer day that you want to suck dry. Travis and Michael and some of the older kids had procured beer; one each was all they could get, so they sipped them slowly and left them carefully in the sand as they went for one last swim.

If Wyatt was being honest, he'd admit that he'd felt left behind. Michael and Travis were crossing a bridge into a world he wasn't invited to, even if he'd wanted to go. It was as if a line had been drawn, and he woke up one day and was stuck with the little kids, no longer part of their crew.

"They think they're so cool," said Sam, watching the older kids in the water. She was braiding her hair, just the front piece, black ropes intertwining away from her face. He may have thought she was beautiful then, or he may have just tried not to because, well, weird.

"They're not," he said.

"It's okay if you want to go in. You're not staying here to babysit me, are you?"

"You're not a baby, Sam."

"Let's dump their beers," she said, jumping up. "Quick. Just Trav and Michael's, and we'll run. They can't tell on us, because they're not supposed to have them anyway." Her hands were on her hips, her left foot tapping.

Wyatt was used to ignoring Sam's sudden, poorly thought-out ideas, but he was just the right amount of resentful to like this one. He leaned forward and took each of their half-full beers and thrust them headfirst into the sand.

When he looked up, the crew of older kids was coming

out of the ocean. Sam grabbed his arm and said, "Run!" They ran up the beach, into and through the dunes, and heard their names being called, and not in a friendly way. Wyatt looked over his shoulder and saw Travis and Michael thirty feet behind them. On the other side of his pool was a small cupboard where they kept the cushions when it rained. The door was half open. Sam saw it the second he did, and they ran to it and slammed the door behind them.

It smelled of sand and salt and wet. They couldn't fit shoulder to shoulder so he had to turn sideways toward her to fit, his knees at his chest. Maybe that had made all the difference, being that close to her and having to look. She smiled at him and her face opened up. He'd seen this smile before, when she found a particularly good haul of shells or when he caught a firefly in a jar and finally agreed to let it go.

She said, "I don't care how mad they get," just as Wyatt heard Travis's voice no more than two feet from the cupboard. So he did it: he placed his fingers on her lips to quiet her. A normal person, he thought many times after, would have placed a finger on his own lips to convey the same message. But he'd chosen to touch hers. It wasn't much, but it was the beginning of everything.

5

Sam

The beach was for bare feet. If Sam had any guiding principle around which she lived her life, it was that. For nine months in Manhattan she was bound up in socks and sneakers. Even during swim season when she raced for the YMCA, she had to wear flip-flops around the pool so she didn't get a wart. But the second they went through the Midtown Tunnel in mid-June, Sam kicked off her shoes.

The beach was for getting up and putting on a bathing suit first thing. It was for grabbing a Pop-Tart and eating it as you raced through the dunes into the ocean while the sun was still low and the gulls were just starting to heat up their wings. Sam was baffled that at fifteen Travis wasted the entire morning sleeping, while she wandered in and out of the ocean, swimming south down the shore and collecting shells. If she found a particularly compelling shell, she'd tuck it under the elastic of her bathing suit and swim the rest of the way to the wooded cove at the south end of the beach. She brought her best shells there, the standouts, and placed them at the base of her favorite linden tree. She knew from experience that if she brought something too interesting home, it would end up as part of one of her mother's art projects. And the beach was for keeping something for herself.

At the beach, she had her own room. It was the most luxurious thing she could imagine after twelve years in the bottom bunk with Travis snoring right over her head. She could stay up and read as long as she wanted without anyone complaining about the light. Sometimes she slept naked just because she could and luxuriated in the feel of the sheets touching every inch of her skin.

Sam was happy to spend time with whoever showed up at the beach each day. If Wyatt was up early, he would come with her as she swam down to the cove. She liked swimming with Wyatt because he was a year older and faster than she was. He followed her out of the water when she wanted to stop and look for shells and waited silently as she inspected whatever had washed up. Sam liked how Wyatt didn't talk unless he had something to say.

"Help me arrange these so they look like they just landed here," Sam said one morning when they'd made it to the base of the linden tree. She'd pulled four shells out of her bathing suit and was pacing the length of the tree, deciding where to put them in relation to the ones she'd placed yesterday. "They're starting to look too organized."

"This is so weird, Sam," Wyatt said, trying to find a patch of sun in the woods where he could dry off.

She was on her hands and knees, turning the shells so they caught the light in different directions. She stood up and admired her design, which was at best abstract but did look as if all of those shells had washed up on a single wave. "Maybe. But it's beautiful." She smiled at him with hands on hips, daring him to disagree. The beach was for following crazy ideas wherever they led.

Wyatt rolled his eyes. "Race you back." And they ran the length of the cove back into the ocean.

At twelve years old, Sam's body was magic. She was a strong swimmer in the pool, but in the ocean she could just let her body go without having to remember to turn around every fifty meters. It seemed like, at the beach, her body knew exactly what to do. The bottoms of her feet toughened as the sand heated up each week. Her body temperature knew how to acclimate as she placed her feet and then her shins in the icy Atlantic. By the time she was fully submerged, she felt indistinguishable from the ocean. Her body felt so right in the summer that it stretched and grew until the straps of her bathing suits left deep marks on her shoulders.

When Wyatt reached over and touched her lips at the end of that summer, she felt something different. She was curious about why his fingers felt so good on her mouth. She almost asked him to keep them there, but the point was to try to be quiet.

6

Wyatt

Wyatt started high school that fall, and it all hit the fan. He knew he couldn't read, at least not like other kids, but he'd faked it by listening to audiobooks or by paying enough attention in class to get by without reading the textbook. His middle school teachers had remarked that he wasn't a strong writer, a generous assessment that he'd earned by being a strong charmer. But in the ninth grade there was no more faking it. His history teacher suggested he be tested, and it all started to fall apart.

In January, he started at a boarding school for kids with learning differences. It was called the Center for Untapped Potential, which Wyatt found patronizing and also a little off. He was skeptical about the idea that his potential was hidden in rural Illinois behind thick brick walls. He knew that, to the extent he had potential, it would be found outdoors, someplace where there was surfing.

He settled into his single room and made friends with the boys on his hall. But by mid-February, when the sky was low and it was dark at four p.m., he stopped trying. He was no longer interested in playing cards. He stopped going to class. He stopped crossing the frozen quad to eat the too-creamy food. By the time the administration figured out that he'd stopped getting out of bed, it had been three days. His parents were called and agreed that he needed counseling.

"Sweetie, it's probably just the weather," Marion said on the phone. "Seasonal affective disorder, it's so common. I'm sending a special light for your room to help with that, and in the meantime you need to go see Dr. Nick. Otherwise, they're going to send you home."

"Promise?" Wyatt said. Florida in February was suddenly a threat?

"I know. I know you want to come home. But this school is the best in the country for helping kids like you. Learn what you can, so that you can come home and finish high school here. Finish the semester, we'll have a fun summer, then we'll talk about another year."

Wyatt slept through his first appointment with Dr. Nick. He was sleeping all the time. But on the morning of his second appointment, the headmaster banged on his door and dragged him into the hall and across campus in his pajama bottoms to the Student Health building.

"So what's been going on?" Dr. Nick was deliberately casual and approachable in jeans and a Van Halen T-shirt. There was an acoustic guitar leaning on his desk. The whole thing looked like a costume to Wyatt, and he imagined Dr. Nick going home and changing into a tweed blazer after work.

"I stopped dealing."

"With what?"

Wyatt looked out the window; he didn't even feel like dealing with the stupid questions about what he wasn't dealing with. "Learning, doing, being, eating. Talking."

"Is there anything you like doing?"

Wyatt took in the endless field of dirty snow. "Surfing. Picked a great spot for it, right?"

He was due back the next day and showed up of his own volition to avoid the spectacle with the headmaster.

"Do you like music?"

"Everyone likes music."

"I see you eyeing my guitar, do you play?"

"No. I just like to listen to music. Like anyone."

"What's that like?"

Wyatt rolled his eyes. "What's it like to listen to music? Same as it is for anyone. I close my eyes and listen. I can see the different instruments coming in and out of the song. I like to pick it apart, I guess."

"That's not the same as it is for anyone."

Wyatt let out a breath. "Great, we've discovered a new area where I'm a freak."

Over the course of two weeks, they talked about how he thought Michael was partying too much. How he thought his parents either were scared of Michael or had given up on him. They talked about Sam and Travis and how their family was perfect, how easy everything was for them. Wyatt described the braid Sam made in the front of her hair, the ease of it.

"I have no idea why I told you that." Wyatt eyed the guitar.

"Listen," said Dr. Nick. "Between you and me, I don't think there's anything wrong with you. I think you're a surfer stuck in the middle of the country in February. I think you might be a little in love with this Sam person." He held up a hand against Wyatt's protest. "But that's your problem, not mine, to fix. I'm going to release you from these sessions, if you agree to my terms."

Wyatt wasn't so sure he wanted to meet the terms; he kind of liked coming to Dr. Nick's office. He still hadn't talked about the thing between his parents, and he felt like he finally wanted to.

"I need you to go to class. Every class. I need you to eat. And every night after dinner, you are going to go to the music department for guitar lessons. First one's tonight. Take this." He handed Wyatt his guitar. Wyatt ran his hand along the smooth neck and let his fingers rest on the frets. He dared to pluck out a sound, and he saw it take shape the second he heard it.

7

Sam

The summer that Sam was fifteen she found herself safely tucked into a group of girls. They gathered on the beach in the late mornings and went to town or to each other's houses when it got too hot. In the afternoons they'd swim or watch the boys surf until the sun went down.

There was a lot of talking in a big group of girls, and Sam tried to keep up. They talked about the boys on the beach, whom they simultaneously ignored and hoped would come talk to them. Every time the talking slowed down, Sam jumped in with a suggestion: swim out to the jetty, dig a hole big enough for all of them, bike to the bakery.

She still spent her mornings with Wyatt, swimming down to the cove and adding shells to her design. They never made plans to do this, but Sam would walk out onto her back deck each morning and find Wyatt sitting on the steps waiting for her.

"Hey," he'd say, getting up.

"Hey," she'd say, and they'd walk straight through the dunes and into the ocean.

On a morning in August, Sam came out for their swim with half a granola bar and a frown. "You okay?" Wyatt asked.

"I'm fine," said Sam, and walked past him through the dunes. She really didn't want to talk about it. Last night her closest girlfriend, Cayla, had called her and said that all of the girls were going to go to a boy's house in Sunnydale. His parents were away and there was going to be a party.

"It's going to be like boys and beer and stuff. Not really your scene, but I just wanted to tell you, like not to leave you out."

Sam could have told Cayla that she'd love to go. But the truth was that it wasn't really her scene. She didn't want to go hang out with a bunch of strange boys; she didn't want to drink beer. She just wanted to wake up early and collect shells. As she swam down toward the cove, she wondered what was wrong with her.

Sam swam straight to the cove without stopping. When they were coming out of the ocean, Wyatt stopped to catch his breath. "God, Sam. The only way I can do this is if you take breaks to look for shells."

Sam wasn't out of breath at all. "I forgot," she said, and walked into the cove.

Wyatt followed her and watched as she moved a few shells around and then moved them back to where they had been before.

"Let's just go," she said.

"Sam, what's wrong with you?"

She didn't say anything. She looked at her shell

collection carefully strewn around under the tree. She wondered for the first time what her friends would say if they saw this.

"You're right," she said. "This is weird."

Wyatt walked over to her and took her hand. It was the first time he'd ever held her hand, and the feel of it completely distracted Sam from feeling sorry for herself. She felt like the heat from his skin on hers was moving all the way up her arm. She placed her other hand on top of his so she could keep this feeling a little longer.

"Come on," he said. "I'm freezing. Let's dry off." Wyatt let go of her hand, and she followed him to a patch of sun at the edge of the cove. They sat looking up the beach, where the sun was still low on the unspent day.

Sam lay down flat on her back and let the sun warm her up. She felt the last drips of water on her skin evaporate. She could still feel where Wyatt's hand had touched hers. She was afraid that if she opened her eyes, she'd stop feeling these things.

"So are you going to tell me?" Wyatt asked.

"What?"

"Whatever you're thinking about."

"I was just thinking how nice it felt when you were holding my hand." Her eyes were still closed.

Wyatt laughed. "That's not why you're upset."

"No, but it's part of the same basic problem—I'm a total weirdo." She sat up and wrapped her arms around her knees, suddenly aware of herself in a bikini.

"You're not that weird, Sam."

"My friends went to a party last night, like a real party."

"And they didn't invite you?"

"Well they told me about it but assumed I wouldn't want to go. Which I didn't. Because I'm a baby."

Wyatt didn't say anything, which she took as a sure sign that he agreed with her. He started scooping sand onto her feet. "They're getting sunburned."

Sam stared at the growing mound on her feet. His covering her with sand felt like he was touching her again. It felt protective.

Wyatt kept his eyes on the sand. "Trust me, Sam, you don't look like a baby."

Something new fluttered in Sam, but she gave Wyatt a shove.

He smiled at the water.

"Sometimes I just want to go back to playing Capture the Flag," she said.

"That's because you're great at it."

"I am."

"You're like a navy SEAL sneaking out of the water."

"I am." Sam was smiling at the ocean. This was true—she was great at Capture the Flag. She loved the beach. Either her friends would slow down or she'd catch up. And Wyatt would still swim with her every morning.

"I'll race you back," she said. She took his hand and led him to the shore, because she wanted to feel it again.

8

Wyatt

In the summer, there are a lot of last nights. The last night before the first kid leaves, meaning the last night summer is still intact. On the last night before Wyatt's family was heading back to Florida, all the kids had a bonfire on the beach, right in front of Wyatt's house. They sat around the fire on scattered beach chairs and blankets. Wyatt arrived late because the silence between his parents felt particularly charged, and he wanted to help pack up the car and stash the pool toys to smooth things over.

He spotted Sam with her friends but was stopped by Travis and Michael, who, at long last, were offering him a beer. "Did you soothe the savage beast, buddy?" Michael asked.

"At least I packed his car . . . we'll see," said Wyatt, taking a sip. He was surprised at how good this felt, being grouped in with the older guys. He wasn't going to turn to check, but he hoped Sam was looking.

Olivia, a girl Michael knew from the restaurant where he worked, took Wyatt's half-full beer away and gave him a full one. He felt like a celebrity. She pulled him down to sit next to her on a blanket by the fire and started talking about the other girls she worked with. It was almost white noise, a series of stories about small sins and failures that amounted to nothing. Wyatt tried to concentrate as the second half of a beer loosened him up. He wondered what Sam and her friends were talking about.

When he finally turned to look, he saw Sam get up, grab her towel, and walk back toward the dunes. She was headed home, and he was leaving at seven the next morning. He sat for a second watching her, knowing he'd get shit from his friends if he went after her, but also not understanding why she wasn't saying goodbye. *She might be coming back*, he thought, but he couldn't risk it.

He got up and followed her onto the narrow path between the tall grasses of the dunes. "Hey," he said, and she didn't stop. "Sam. Wait."

She stopped and he caught up with her, her head still down. "What?"

"Are you leaving? You know I'm leaving tomorrow. I wanted to say goodbye." She was still looking down. He put his hand on her shoulder. "You okay?"

When she looked up, there were tears in her eyes. "It's just . . . The summer's over. You're leaving. And suddenly you're a jerk with a beer and you've just left me already."

"Sam, you know I was going to come talk to you. I always come talk to you." His hand was still on her shoulder. "You're my person on the beach."

Sam wiped her eyes with the back of her hand. "I'm being stupid. I'm just sad."

"Let's be in better touch this year. Like text me some-times and tell me what you're reading, and I'll tell you how boring it sounds."

"Okay," she said.

"Are you really going home already?" The thought of it was excruciating to him.

"Yeah, I'm not into all that out there." She looked up at him, and this next part would live in his memory in super slow motion: her hair fell over her eye, the piece that she sometimes braided. He took his hand from her shoulder and touched it and brushed it away behind her ear. Now his hand was on her neck and his heart was racing and he had to stop this right now before he ruined everything.

And that's when she kissed him. At first it felt like she was testing it out, brushing her lips against his to see what that might feel like. Then it was a slow, warming-up kiss that he wanted to dive all the way into. He kept his hand on her neck and pulled her to him with his free arm. When their bodies were touching, Sam pulled away.

"Okay, now I'm embarrassed. I have no idea why I did that and I need to go home."

"Sam." He pulled her into a hug and buried his face in her hair.

"No, really, I'm going to be so weird if I stay here. I'm sorry, I don't know what my problem is."

Wyatt smiled at her, feeling suddenly in control of things. "Sam, it's nothing. Just text me tomorrow. I'll be bored in the car." She hugged him again and walked toward her house. It wasn't nothing.

9

Sam

The next morning, Sam came back from swimming alone to find that Wyatt had texted her the minute his family started their drive back to Florida. It was basic chitchat, his wondering how the waves were, saying how boring the ride was. Sam felt a layered wave of relief, both that texting with Wyatt wasn't disappearing with the summer and that her kissing him (like a total lunatic, she would have added if she had anyone to tell) wasn't going to make things weird. Wyatt was a true friend and she wasn't going to let her completely out-of-control body do anything to compromise that.

By the time they were both back in school, they were texting every day. It was a strange thing to bring her summer person back into the city in this way. She texted him on the subway and from the locker room at the YMCA. They no longer needed the surf report as an excuse to text, and it felt like the more they talked, the more there was to say. Wyatt told her about songs he was writing. He told her he'd play them for her next summer. He told her about how his parents didn't speak directly to one another for the entirety of parents' weekend. Sam told him about how her geometry teacher hated her and that the girls in her grade were sneaking into clubs. Sam's favorite part of the day was getting into bed at night, because she usually heard from him then. She smiled at her phone every time the first text came in: What's happening in the big city?

It was during winter break, when Wyatt was in Florida and Sam was in New York, that he came clean about his school. Travis was out, so Sam was taking advantage of being able to actually talk on the phone in their room.

"I need to tell you something." He sounded really nervous. "I've been sort of lying."

"What?" Sam said. *He has a girlfriend.* This thought landed with a thud. It had never occurred to her before. Why wouldn't Wyatt have a girlfriend? One who could also play the guitar at his artsy school. The hand that held the phone to her ear felt shaky, and she braced it with her other hand while she waited.

"My school is for kids with learning differences. I have dyslexia. But I do play music there. I just felt weird that you didn't know."

Waves of relief. Like all the way through her body. Sam let out a breath.

"Does it bother you?" he asked.

"Why would it bother me?"

"Well, like, all you do is read. And it's the thing I can't do."

"Yeah, because our whole friendship is based on books? Who cares?" He may have interpreted Sam's light tone as compassion. But really she was just so happy he didn't have a girlfriend.

ONE FRIDAY NIGHT, Wyatt texted at midnight. Sam smiled when she saw it was him, that familiar but impossible feeling that he was in bed with her.

Wyatt: Hey

Sam: It's late. What are you doing?

Wyatt: I was just down the hall drinking screwdrivers with some kids

Sam: You could get in so much trouble

Wyatt: I know. But it was fun

Sam: Okay, but be careful

Wyatt: Do you think you'll ever kiss me again?

It was March by then. They'd talked about every other thing in the world, but never that kiss. Sam stared at her phone. She was taking too long to reply. Her heart was racing, and her mind was going blank. Her friends would have been able to think of the cool thing to say. She could only say the truth: I hope so.

Wyatt: Me too. Goodnight

10

Wyatt

Wyatt's junior year of high school felt full. He was spending two hours a day in the music department, and he joined the swim team for the feel of the cold water on his skin. He was learning strategies for decoding words that made him a better, if slow, reader. Plus, he had a girlfriend. Well, not really, but he had Sam in his life nearly every day, and the whole thing had potential.

When the Popes pulled into their driveway on Saltaire Lane at the end of May, Sam was in the front yard. She was sixteen, in cut-off shorts and a tank top and no shoes. Her hair was longer and was pulled back in a ponytail. Just that one strand hung loose in the front, and Wyatt wondered if it was on purpose.

"Hi." She waved as Marion and Frank, Michael, and finally Wyatt got out of the car.

"Well, you look all grown up, Sam," said Frank.

"It's creepy," said Michael, grabbing two suitcases and heading to the house.

Marion gave her a hug. "Don't listen to him. I'm so happy to be here, we'll have a great summer."

When Marion had gone into the house, it was just Wyatt and Sam on the front lawn, six feet between them, which might as well have been a thousand.

"So hey," Sam started. "Why is this awkward?"

Wyatt laughed. He could always count on Sam to just say it. "I don't know, because we're not used to being in real life? You look different."

Sam looked down at herself and back at Wyatt. "You do too, but in a good way."

"I mean it in a good way too, Sam," Wyatt said. Frank called from inside, something about taking the pool cover off. "I'll see you later," he said, and hoped it sounded cool.

THE HOLLOWAYS INVITED the Popes for a barbecue on the back porch. Wyatt had eaten there dozens of times before, and there was a formula for it. Bill grilled some kind of protein, and Laurel served some kind of creamy carbohydrate and a salad. There was always a basket of bread on the table and a room-temperature stick of butter, to make it easier to spread. Over Wyatt's entire childhood he'd marveled at how easy things were at the Holloways' house. Who thinks to leave the butter out to soften? Wyatt's mom didn't like to cook and mostly heated things up, things that Frank found too salty and unevenly heated. There were entire dinners devoted to this line of conversation, just how bad the food was.

This night, the official first night of summer because they were all together, the table twinkled with candlelight. The meal was steaks, macaroni and cheese, and an arugula salad. As always, the kids sat at one end of the table, but this year it felt more like they were almost all adults. Travis and Michael were nineteen, Travis having just finished his first year at Trinity College; Michael was at the University of Miami. Wyatt was seventeen, and Bill offered him a glass of wine. He'd never forget it, this rite of a passage, or anything about this night.

Sam and Wyatt sat next to each other at the table, comfortable in the fact that they didn't really have to look at one another unless they did so deliberately. When they did turn to face one another they were so close that they quickly looked away. Wyatt's shoulder occasionally brushed up against Sam's, and eventually he just let it rest there against hers. Bill asked questions up and down the table— how was Frank's golf game this winter? What was Marion going to do about the Asian shore crabs that were moving toward her yard? What did Michael think about the Dolphins? When he got to Wyatt, it was about college, of course.

"I'm not really sure," he said. "I want to go out to Los Angeles and work in music."

"So like USC? UCLA?" Bill asked. It was an innocent question, but Wyatt knew for sure at that moment that his parents hadn't told their best friends about his learning situation.

"Someplace around there." Wyatt smiled generally at the table, in the way he did when he wanted to smooth things over.

Marion jumped in to change the subject. "Well, you're not going anywhere until you get that treehouse cleaned out or just take the whole eyesore down."

"Over my dead body," said Frank. "Taking it down, I mean."

AFTER DINNER, THE four kids ran down to the ocean for a night swim. The moon was low and cast a long white stripe on the water. Wyatt was torn between enjoying the exquisite chill of the water rising up his legs and trying not to look at Sam in her red bikini. She'd worn bikinis last summer, but they had been sportier somehow. This one had actual strings on her hips and on her back. He was mesmerized by them dangling in the water, the invitation to pull one and watch all that fabric float away.

When they got out of the ocean, Michael and Travis went down the beach to smoke a joint. Wyatt wondered if this was the progression of things, if next summer he and Sam would be smoking pot too. He didn't like the idea of Sam smoking pot.

Wyatt and Sam sat on the sand wrapped in their towels, watching them walk away. "Losers," Sam said.

"Really," said Wyatt.

"So, you don't seem to have so much to say to me now that we're actually together. We're still friends, right?" She was looking down at the sand, drawing a circle with her hand. The moon lit up her face in such a way that he could see each freckle on her nose. There was the tiniest bit of sand in her eyelashes. She looked up at him. "Right?"

"Of course, we're friends. Am I being weird? I think I need to get used to you."

"You're not used to me? You've known me your whole life."

I need to get used to how I want to pull on that red string, Wyatt didn't say. *Used to the way I actually need to touch your lips.* Sam was acting mildly rejected, and Wyatt didn't have the confidence to set her straight. He felt incapable of self-regulation, like if he opened up about how he was feeling it would rush out and drown them both.

NOW

11

Jack's still reading, and it's possible that he'll finish this book before I get through the first chapter. This doesn't worry me because with Jack staying over the garage I can stay up late to catch up. I like the way reading these books feels so deliberate, like each page requires my full attention to take in and process the words. It's sort of like muscle confusion, but for the mind.

Kids are building sandcastles on the beach, and teenagers are sprawled out on towels waiting for a swell. Wyatt is playing the guitar in his treehouse. All the characters have reassembled on this beach after fourteen years, and I am the only thing that's different.

Gracie runs outside in a yellow one-piece bathing suit that may have been mine a hundred years ago. "Sammy, let's go for a swim." Before I can respond, she's grabbed my hand and is pulling me up from my chair. "We're at the beach. Put on a bathing suit." Hands on hips, Gracie is exasperated by my beach incompetence.

"Fine," I say, and go upstairs to change while Gracie

yells through my window for me to hurry up. The urgency in her voice reminds me of a time when a beach day felt so exciting that I didn't want to waste a single second of it.

When I'm back on the deck, she grabs my hand, and we walk through the dunes, the ones where I kissed Wyatt for the first time. "Are you going to talk to him?" Gracie asks, motioning to the treehouse.

"Not on purpose," I say. "How long has he been here?"

"Like a month."

"He's been here for a whole month? Is he homeless or something?"

"Doesn't seem like it."

We slog through the hot sand and pass a towel island full of girls a few years older than Gracie. She steers clear of their too-loud laughter, their too-small bikinis. I try to remember being twelve, still wearing board shorts and a rash guard and trying to hang out with my brother, eyeing the older girls like they were an exotic disease I was about to catch.

I drop my towel, roll my sunglasses into my cover-up, and cover the bundle with my hat. Gracie is already running into the water. I follow her and my feet are wet, waves retreating and then racing up my calves. I wade out to where Gracie is already fully submerged, and suddenly I am also twelve years old. Weightless, unencumbered, and free. Beyond the waves, Gracie and I float on our backs and she reaches for my hand, unselfconscious in that naïve way where you still think nothing will ever change.

Gracie's a strong swimmer, and I like to take credit for it. When she was two years old and I was at NYU, I started

taking her to swimming classes at the YMCA. The mothers
looked at me with concern and a touch of horror—practically
a teenager myself with no wedding ring and a two-year-old
on my hip. *Nothing to see here,* I always wanted to tell them,
she's just my emotional support toddler. Dr. Judy assured me
I'd get past this, but after Wyatt and I broke up, the only
thing that brought me back to myself was Gracie. Holding
Gracie in the water. Taking Gracie for a too-big sundae at
Serendipity. Turning my old bedroom into a safari and taking a Sharpie to our pajamas so that we could be leopards.
Gracie's unfiltered joy should come in pill form.

We swim south along the horizon toward the cove until
my limbs are jelly and I call for her to stop. "My sister is an
old lady," she laughs as we wade out of the water about an
eighth of a mile from our house.

"Kind of," I say, catching my breath and shaking out
my hair. I can't even see where my towel is as we walk along
the shore, and I can't remember the last time I just walked
around in a bathing suit, the sun drying the salt and sand on
my skin. "Maybe I should hang out with you more."

"We should hang out here more," she says. "Even Jack
seems to like it here, right?"

I don't answer because there's someone standing by my
towel; he's stuck his surfboard in the sand. I stop. Or my
feet stop; I don't even know if I mean to stop. But Gracie is
running toward him. He lifts a hand in a wave and I know
I need to be an adult here. It's been thirteen summers.

I start walking and am more acutely aware than ever of
how awkward it is to walk across soft sand in a bathing suit.
There's the fact of your whole body's being fully exposed

from all angles in the horrific light of day, combined with
the up-and-down jiggly motion of sand stepping. I chose a
bikini from my childhood dresser, red with a triangle top
and side-tie bottoms, so that I can keep the new ones I
bought for my honeymoon pristine. What good are those
bikinis doing me now, all wrapped up in tissue? Of all the
bad decisions that have led me to this moment, the one that
caused me to be approaching Wyatt with my thirty-year-old
body shoved into the bikini of my youth is the baddest.

"Hey, Sam-I-am," Wyatt says like it's nothing. The
sound of his voice is like a song on the radio that takes you
back in time with the first few notes. It hits me right in the
chest and moves throughout my body. My hand flies up to
my neck to wipe away the memory of his lips there.

"Hey," I say. He's tan. His hair is a slightly darker shade
of brown, longish and brushed off his face as if it's been
combed back by fingers. He's smiling just a little bit and
there are laugh lines by his eyes. I stare at these lines, a bit
stunned by my own stupidity. In my mind Wyatt is seventeen, sitting by me on the beach waiting for waves. Then
he's eighteen and actively not returning my calls. That's
where I lost track of him. And now here he is, thirty-one,
with his more defined jawline and his filled-in frame. Of
course Wyatt grew up.

His bathing suit seems new, which is all wrong, because
I'm the one who's moved on. It is of critical importance to
my inner teenager that he knows I've moved on. If I could
think of a way to bring up my 401(k), I would.

"So, I hear you're getting married out here," he says.

"Maybe," I say. "Or in Connecticut. We haven't decided. Jack and I. My fiancé. Jack." *Oh my God, stop.*

"He's a lucky guy," he says, which gives me pause. Wyatt was a lucky guy. Wyatt left me. How lucky could he
possibly think Jack is?

"He is," I say. "A little old for a treehouse, aren't you?"
I don't know where to put my arms and they seem to be trying out every possible location. Hands on my hips, arms
across my chest, hands clasped behind my back. It's like I'm
doing my own version of the Macarena.

Wyatt looks at Gracie. "Not really."

"You should climb up and see it," she says. "It's awesome."

"I've seen it," I say, and feel my face go hot. "We should
get inside. I'm getting sunburned." I throw on my cover-up,
which I can't believe I didn't do earlier. "Nice to see you.
Come on, Gracie."

WHEN WE'RE BACK on the porch, my mom is leaning
over the railing like she's been watching. She gives me a look
and I shake my head. *No, don't worry, I'm fine. No, I don't
want to talk about it. No, I'm not still in love with the boy who
broke my heart in high school.*

Jack doesn't look up from his book, but I squeeze in
next to him on the lounge chair, arranging his arm around
me and resting my head on his chest. Jack's body feels solid,
like a house that's well cared for and overly insured.

"You're getting sunburned," he says, pulling away.

"It's not contagious," I say.

"It's not funny, you have freckles coming out over your nose just from this morning's exposure."

I put on my hat, and Jack lets out a breath. I settle my head on his chest. I've moved on to a much better place.

12

I wake up Sunday morning to a rather formal email from Eleanor telling me that I am on leave for the week while management reviews my employment status. I am not to come into the office until notified by an officer of Human Corps. Eleanor isn't just my boss, she's my friend. We've been out for drinks together, we've gotten manicures. I know which one of her kids doesn't eat dairy and which one needs an EpiPen. And now, reading this email, she feels like a human corpse.

We could still leave tomorrow morning. We've done our three days. But there's a hint of relief in the idea of not going back to the city, of swimming in the ocean and taking Jack to see Starfish Beach. Jack seems happy and relaxed out here and I don't know what I was so afraid of. I wonder if, without Wyatt here, this is a place where we could return as a married couple. Our kids running in and out of the water all day.

My mom considers it a major victory when I tell her we're staying for another few days. "I knew it," she says, and I'm not sure what she knew. We decide to push off our visit to the Old Sloop Inn because Jack hasn't been to the gym in two days. We have plenty of time, so it's totally fine with me. He finds Mom, Granny, and me on the back porch.

"I'm going to combine push day with leg day, to make up for yesterday," he tells me. "Want to meet in town for lunch?"

"Sure," I say. "Let's meet at Chippy's at noon."

"You won't forget?"

I give him a little swat. "No, I'll be hungry, so my stomach will remind me."

He kisses me on the top of my head, and I have this familiar warm feeling as I watch him walk away, like I'm dating the captain of the football team.

"Why would you forget lunch?" my mom asks.

"He's just teasing me. I've been forgetting things. Like I missed our ballroom dancing lesson."

"Ballroom dancing?" Granny asks. "Who are you?"

My mom laughs. "For the wedding. It's nice to see a bride and groom who can waltz."

"Exactly. But I got caught up at work and totally forgot. Two weeks in a row."

Granny narrows her eyes at me. "Interesting."

"Not really. I have a wedding coming up and nothing's been planned. I have a pretty intense job. I mean, it's normal that I would let something slip through the cracks."

"What else have you forgotten?" Granny asks in a tone that's reminiscent of Dr. Judy.

I shrug. Besides forgetting to keep my big mouth shut at work, I can't think of anything. "Nothing."

Granny says, "You might want to consider the fact that on some level you don't want to waltz."

My mom says, "Mother, that's ridiculous. Every bride wants to waltz." It's probably true. I like the idea of Jack and me moving perfectly in step, one-two-three, one-two-three, around the dance floor. How relaxing it would be if there were choreography for everything.

"It's unbelievable that, of the three of us, I'm the one they call old," Granny says.

"Laurel?" It's Wyatt's voice coming from the other side of the hedge.

"Over here," my mom replies. And there he is, coming out of the dunes and up the porch steps.

I pull my cover-up over my not-so-tan thighs and reach for sunglasses that aren't there. I know my mother sees.

He walks onto the deck and looks around. "Boy, I haven't been here in a long time."

"Well we've missed you," says my mom, a traitor. "Can I get you some iced tea?" Iced tea. After all that happened. We're going to sit down and have some iced tea.

"Thanks, but I can't. I'm headed over to the Owl Barn to help set up for the festival, and I had to take my mom's car in for an inspection. Travis left me his car, but I don't see the keys." It hurts a little to see Wyatt as a still-aspiring musician who's driving a borrowed car. Not that I have a car, but I feel like Wyatt should.

"Ah, they're in the kitchen in the bowl by the sink," my mom says.

"Thanks," Wyatt says to my mother. "I'll drop the keys by later."

Granny takes a sip of her tea. My mom folds back the brim of her sun hat. Wyatt is looking at me.

"What?" I hear myself say.

He smiles, new lines by his eyes but the same soft smile.

"Nothing. It's just been a really long time. And I'm trying to decide how you're different."

I really wish I had sunglasses. "I'll save you some time. I'm different in every single way."

"I don't think so." And he walks right into my house.

THEN

13

Wyatt

The waves were never that great right in front of Wyatt's house, but he liked to ride a few in the late morning anyway. He'd been surfing for so long that his board felt like an extension of him, and each wave felt like an opening. So much of his life had been filled with things that felt impossible— reading, math, even existing peacefully in his family. Being out on the water felt completely natural, and he wondered if his whole life could be filled with things that felt easy and made sense. Surfing, playing the guitar. Sam.

He got out of the water and found Sam in the middle of a big group, laughing. There was something about the way Sam laughed that always made Wyatt want to stop and watch. She didn't laugh as a punctuation to something she'd just said or because the people around her were laughing. Sam laughed because something was really funny, so funny that it scrunched up her face and shook her shoulders. Sam was a person who was capable of giving herself up to her laughter, and as he stood and watched, he thought it might be his favorite thing.

Sam looked over and caught his eye. A few kids turned to see him just standing there, wet with his board. He had to say something because, otherwise, he was just a guy standing there, staring.

"I'm going to teach you to surf," he said.

Sam jumped up. "Okay. Let me get Travis's board," she said, as if these were plans they already had.

When they were out on the water, Sam paddled next to him. "This is kind of hard," she said, thrusting herself through the water.

"You'll get used to it," he said, pulling ahead. They paddled over small swells to where it was completely still.

They lay facedown on their boards, and Wyatt reached out to hold on to Sam's board so they wouldn't float apart. There was an intimacy in this huge expanse of space, even more so than when they'd been hiding in that storage cabinet, or that time he'd passed her on the narrow stairs on his way to Travis's room. They weren't as close, but they were intensely alone. There were no waves, so they just floated.

"Have you been writing songs?" she asked, scooping water onto his board.

"Almost constantly."

"About what?"

"Whatever I'm thinking about a lot."

"What do you think about a lot?"

"I don't know, Sam." He was flustered. She was what he thought about a lot. The way she smiled at him, the spot where her neck curved into her shoulder. The way he wanted to reach out and touch her all the time but didn't want to risk making things weird and losing her. "Stupid stuff mostly. If I write anything good, I'll play it for you."

"Okay, geez." Sam splashed him. "Are you really going to teach me to surf?"

"Do you really want to learn?" He loved being alone with Sam on the water, and if he could get her to start surfing, they could do this all the time.

"No," Sam said.

"Yes you do."

Sam laughed. "I'd like to be able to surf, it seems fun. But I am not going to try to stand up on this thing and fall flat on my face a hundred times."

"You'd be a great surfer."

"Because you think I can jump up into the air and land on a piece of wiggling fiberglass?"

"I do."

Sam looked out at the horizon and back at the kids on the beach. "If you really think so."

"I can't teach you out here, especially with no waves. We'll start on solid ground and I'll teach you to pop up. Tomorrow morning at eight. Meet me at the beach."

14

Sam

Surfing was impossible. Impossible, frustrating, and unnecessary. Why not just swim? They started on the sand,
and after two lessons, Sam mastered the motion of popping
up. But in the water, the variables were too much for her.
She would pop up perfectly just as a small swell came and
threw her off-balance.

"I can't do this," she said, pulling her board back toward her and climbing on.

"Of course you can."

"The water keeps moving."

"That's what water does, Sam. Get back up."

They met each morning, and Sam tried. She'd sit on her
board and watch as Wyatt rode wave after wave, like it was
nothing.

After a particularly inelegant fall, Sam sat on her board,
braiding her wet hair, and said, "I give up. The ocean wins."

Wyatt laughed. "That's kind of your problem. You have
a vibe about you like you're trying to compete with the

ocean. This isn't a win/lose thing. It's like you need to adjust to the movement of the ocean, to cooperate."

"Oh my God, stop," Sam said.

"Just try to catch a wave like you're not trying so hard. Get up and then be fully willing to fall off. I mean you're already wet, right?"

Sam knew he was right. Everything she loved to do came without force. She'd become a swimmer gradually. She'd started drawing without any particular end in mind. She opened books and just let them carry her away. The most fun she ever had happened when she acted on an idea without thinking it through. But trying to surf felt like trying to master gravity. She wasn't entirely proud of the feelings that came up when she was considering a wave: distrust, uncertainty, fear. She liked the way Wyatt thought of her as strong and capable, the girl who could always capture the flag.

The next morning she got out to the beach at seven. There were small waves breaking in front of her house and she figured she had nothing to lose. She wanted to feel what it was like to glide along the curl of a wave, staying steady but open enough to let it take her wherever it was going. Something was happening to her, and it scared her, mostly the fact that her body acted of its own accord around Wyatt. She wanted to be open enough to let that take her, too.

The water was cold on her feet, cool on her shins, and then absolutely perfect once she was all the way in. Her body knew what it was doing. She paddled out to where the waves were breaking and waited for the right wave and her courage to emerge at the same time. A wave started forming from the south and she decided to try. She pushed up and felt the board beneath her feet. She imagined the motion beneath her went both ways, as if the ocean moved her and she moved the ocean. She was completely underwater before she realized she'd ridden that wave.

She came up for air and saw Wyatt running into the waves to meet her. "I saw it!" he called to her. He held out his arms like he was going to hug her but dropped them to his sides quickly. To her own surprise, she threw her arms around his neck. He hugged her back, and the feel of him, warm and dry, pressed against her wet body, was shocking. It had never occurred to her that another person's skin against hers could make her feel like she was melting. Her skin felt so soft against his that she wondered if it had been changed somehow, as if the cells of his body interacted with hers to create a whole other thing. Wyatt let go first, which embarrassed her, like he'd been standing there waiting for it to be over.

"So you snuck out here and taught yourself to surf?"

"I guess. I don't know how it happened." She was relieved he'd changed the subject. She was afraid she might ask him how his skin felt against hers. She wanted to know.

"Let's go back out," he said. He hopped on his board and started to paddle. He was smiling.

15

Sam

"I have a great idea," said Sam to the kids on the beach.

"Here we go," said Cayla.

Sam ignored her. This really was a great idea. "Let's camp out down at the cove tonight. All of us. Sleeping bags and s'mores and stuff. The weather's good. And if there are waves in the morning, we can surf first thing."

Everyone liked the idea, and they agreed to meet on the beach before sunset so they could walk down to the cove and arrive as it got dark. Sam didn't have any particular feeling about sleeping outside, but the idea of being there in the dark with her friends and then watching the sky brighten first thing gave her the feeling that she was taking summer to a whole new level.

Sam and Wyatt found themselves walking ahead of the pack with their surfboards and sleeping bags. He was wearing a Chicago Cubs T-shirt that had been washed the exact number of times it took to make it rest perfectly over the outline of his chest. Sam had noticed this before, stealing glances at him from the passenger seat of his dad's truck. It was strange, she thought, how distracted she could be by his body in that T-shirt when she spent half the day with him in no T-shirt at all. Wyatt shirtless looked great, but Wyatt in that T-shirt was obscene.

They dropped their sleeping bags in the woods, and Sam and Wyatt pretended to be surprised to see the array of shells surrounding the big linden tree. "Looks like they all came in on a single wave," said Wyatt. Everyone agreed, though no one was very interested.

The sun wasn't quite down, and everyone scattered around the cove to watch it set. Sam was watching the orange sky move into purple from behind the branches of the linden tree when she felt Wyatt come and stand behind her. She turned around and touched the bottom of his T-shirt. This was another thing she didn't think through, her hand just wanted to run the fabric between her finger and thumb. She imagined she could feel where it was still warm from resting against his skin. She wanted to touch his stomach. She knew that you can't just go around touching people's stomachs, but now her whole body wanted her to run her fingertips over his abdomen. It terrified her. She looked up and he was watching her.

"I have a thing for this shirt," she said. "And seriously, Wyatt, I'm the weirdest person ever."

Wyatt smiled, and she turned around to watch the sun finish setting.

16

Wyatt

Wyatt told his mother he would quit surfing early so he could clean out the treehouse, which still hadn't been done three weeks after they'd arrived at the beach, the floor still covered with leaves that had blown in over the past nine months, wet and decayed. But he'd gotten a tune in his head when he was sitting with Sam on the beach earlier, and it repeated like tunes often did when they were trying to get out into the world. He sat down with his guitar just to see if he could capture it. He started slowly and corrected himself a few times before it sounded right. He could see the notes as he heard them, over and over again.

A song was starting to take shape when Sam showed up at the bottom of the rope ladder. He smiled because it was as if she'd walked into his song. She wore jeans, rolled up at the bottom, and a white T-shirt that was the tiniest bit too short, a negligible amount of stomach showing, so little that it could have been a mistake. Her hair was down and still wet from the shower, leaving the shoulders of her T-shirt slightly see-through. It was all too much for Wyatt. He put his guitar down and stood up.

"Not much of a cleaner, are you?" she said at the top of the ladder. She walked past him and grabbed the broom off the floor.

"I got distracted," he said, trying to take it from her.

She lowered her hand on the broom so that their hands were touching. He liked the feel of her hand over his, just that spot where the bottom of her fist touched the top of his.

"What are you doing here?" he said, and it came out too small. They stood there, holding hands around the broom, for what seemed like forever. They were too close to be just talking, but not close enough.

Sam said, "I wanted to see you."

"Yeah," he said. The moon lit up the space and the air between them felt thick. It was a risk to kiss her, but maybe a bigger risk not to. It ached to want something this much. He barely had to move to brush his lips against hers, and he lingered there, just to make sure. Sam kissed him back and wrapped her arms around his neck. After that, something between them took over. It was as if, after taking this step, there was only one path forward. He'd practiced this kiss in his mind a thousand times. But he was not prepared for the salty-sweet taste of Sam's lips and the urgent way she pressed her body against his. His hands were everywhere—her hair, her neck, her hips—as if this were his one chance to touch every part of her.

"We need to slow down," she said by the time they were lying on the damp leaves.

"Do we?" He was not slowing down.

"We have all summer."

I want forever, he thought.

17

Sam

"I really think I should go home," Sam said, because it sounded like the sane thing to say. It came out breathless, and she knew she didn't sound like she meant it. She felt drunk from kissing Wyatt for so long. Just being able to run her hands along his arms and feel his breath on her neck made her wonder if she'd ever have the strength to climb back down the rope ladder.

"Don't," he said, kissing her again. "Or do, I don't know. I just want you to want to come back."

Sam laughed. "I'll come back."

When she finally went home, she couldn't sleep. She wanted to text him, but she couldn't imagine what she would say after all that.

She took out her sketch pad and started drawing. There was an image of Wyatt in her mind from earlier that night, sitting on the edge of the treehouse playing the guitar. It was a song she hadn't heard before, and she'd followed it through the dunes and to the rope ladder. She'd wondered if she should turn back and leave him alone with his song, but she'd wanted to see him. When she was on the third rung of the rope ladder, he looked up at her but continued to play. It was a split second when he was fully immersed in his music and smiling at her at the same time. It was like he'd let her all the way in.

NOW

18

It's Monday and Jack goes for a run before our appointment to see the Old Sloop Inn. I put on a sundress so I can seem bridal, like it's an occasion. Which it is. Outside my bedroom window, my dad is staring at the engine of his old VW Bug, hand resting on the open trunk. He pours money into this car year after year, and it always lets him down. He claims that the sky blue of the paint and the curve of the fender inspired the original *Current*. I think he just doesn't like throwing things out.

Wyatt appears from behind the hedge, and I briefly wonder what good a hedge is if it isn't actually doing its job of keeping us separate. He has his head under the hood now, his toolbox on the ground. I want to hear what they're saying, but I don't want to draw attention to myself by opening the window. It's hard to fathom the two of them together, just shooting the breeze like this. Wyatt is pointing to something and goes in with a wrench. Dad is listening to him, nodding.

Jack returns from his run, a new addition to this silent

movie from hell. From my perch I see them together for the first time. My dad introduces them, and they shake hands. The two loves of my life, so different from one another. Everything about Jack is by design. His body is the result of a specific gym regimen engineered for ultimate fitness. His hair is parted and combed to hang at an exact spot on his neck, cut every three weeks by Pablo on Sixty-Eighth Street. Jack might be the privet of people.

Wyatt is bent over, working. His baseball hat is backward and I know exactly how his hair would pop out if he took it off. The muscles tense in his arms in a functional way. He looks fit from surfing and working with his hands.

Dad gets in the car, turns the key, and there's success. Celebratory smiles and pats on the back all around. My dad is beaming at Wyatt, then Jack, who is considering something. He nods and this odd trio disperses.

"SO YOUR DAD invited Wyatt on our excursion tonight. He seemed like he wanted me to okay it, so I did," Jack tells me.

I pull into the Old Sloop Inn parking lot and find a spot before responding. "Why?"

"I don't know. What was I going to say? 'You can't come because you dated my fiancé when she was a kid'? Plus, it wouldn't hurt to have a mechanic on the boat. I've seen how much your dad knows about fixing a car."

"He's not a mechanic," I say, and I have no idea why.

"He fixed your dad's car. And he says he does a lot of that at a Shell station out in LA."

So Wyatt works at a gas station. It tugs on me a little bit to think he's so far away from where he wanted to be. I never imagined Wyatt doing anything besides playing the guitar. And now here he is, still looking out over the ocean trying to come up with something that will sell. But, whatever. I build productivity graphs, and it's not like that was my dream. When we were kids, my dream was to be at the beach, with Wyatt, forever.

THEN

19

Wyatt

There would never be a better summer. Wyatt knew it the second he kissed Sam. He woke up every morning knowing that he was going to see her and touch her. He couldn't imagine anything better than that. Sam got a job taking care of kids at the library five mornings a week. She'd ride her bike there, and after story time, Duck-Duck-Goose, and Goldfish, Wyatt would meet her with sandwiches and they'd drive to the north end of the beach and eat them on the jetty. Some days they'd throw their surfboards in the back of Frank's old truck and drive around Long Island looking for waves. The only thing Wyatt loved more than kissing Sam was kissing Sam in the ocean. The feel of her wet body against his and the salty taste of her were his new favorite things.

Wyatt worked at the Auto Hop in the mornings, changing oil and occasionally taking apart engines. He loved how a car was a complete unit, built for the express purpose of running. There was only one way for the crankshaft to connect to the rubber belts and the rubber belts to connect to the camshaft. It made sense every time. When he wasn't working or hanging out with Sam, he was writing songs. More accurately, he was writing songs the whole time he was with Sam too, just in his head. Fixing cars, writing songs, being with Sam. It was perfect.

It didn't take long for everyone on the beach to figure out they were a couple. Everyone in town knew too. The waitresses at Chippy's Diner smiled at each other every time they sat down at their regular booth. When they walked into Ginnie's Bakery, Ginnie put her hand over her heart and said, "Oh, it's that sweet young couple!" Sam's boss at the library always called over her shoulder when she saw him outside, "Your Wyatt's here!" He understood that this should have been embarrassing, but he loved being her Wyatt.

Most days they'd find themselves back at the beach after lunch. Sam would surf or sit and catch up with her friends. Wyatt tried to act like a normal person. He tried to hang out with his friends and talk to other people when they were in the larger group, but he always gravitated back to her. He loved when she'd catch his eye across the bonfire at night and smile at him in a way that made him know she was going to sneak out to the treehouse to see him later.

Dinner happened mostly on the Holloways' deck. Wyatt's family was invited several nights a week, as they always had been, just sort of wandering over with wine and something to throw on the grill. These nights with the sun setting over the ocean and his parents exhibiting their outside behavior—polite to each other and charming to everyone else—Wyatt felt the deepest sense of peace he'd ever known. Even Michael came to dinner and was his best self, laughing with Travis or talking about sports with Bill. Wyatt liked the way his family felt when it was part of the Holloways'.

20

Sam

Around midnight on a Thursday in July, Sam was sitting on her bed listening to Wyatt work on a new song in the treehouse. She'd been drawing him there since the first night he kissed her. His legs dangling over the edge, the moon over the water lighting up the space. She'd done eight versions of this drawing and she'd started to think the details of the treehouse didn't matter as much as the opening she'd seen in his eyes. She wanted to crawl right into that space. The first versions of the drawing were overdone, but this was the one she liked best, with the whole scene in outline and only his eyes drawn in intricate detail.

Sam had gone to town for dinner with her parents and then to a movie, an excruciating four hours, which meant she wouldn't see him until tomorrow. She and Wyatt had driven all the way to Garnet Bay earlier in the day, presumably to surf, but had ended up making out in the back of the truck instead.

"That's it," he'd whispered into her ear, the full weight of his body on her.

"That's what?" she asked.

"My favorite sound. It's like you're catching your breath. It's my favorite thing in the world. I'm going to write a song about it."

"You're my favorite thing in the world," Sam said, and, although she knew for a fact this was true and that he already knew it, she felt completely laid bare.

He lifted himself onto his elbow so he could look her in the eye. It was an eternity before he said, "I love you, Sam."

"Are you sure?" she said, mainly because she wanted to hear him say it again.

"I'm pretty sure I've loved you my whole life. But not like this, like I do now."

Sam hadn't heard anything anyone had said at dinner that night. She'd missed the entire point of the movie. She was scheduled to work in the morning, which meant she wouldn't see Wyatt until lunchtime. This seemed impossibly long as she grabbed her finished drawing and made her way downstairs and out the back door and through the dunes to the rope ladder. Wyatt was right where she'd drawn him, brow furrowed and legs dangling.

"I couldn't sleep," she said, sitting next to him.

"Good," he said, and kissed her.

"I drew this. I wanted you to have it." She handed him the drawing and watched him take it in. "I know it doesn't look finished, but I was just trying to get that expression, and I didn't want all the other stuff to take away from it."

"It's incredible," he said.

Sam felt relieved and also kind of embarrassed. "Let's

hang it up." She got up and found a nail sticking out of one of the side walls. "Here?"

"That's going to wreck it," he said. "We can get a frame or something tomorrow."

She loved that she'd created something that mattered to him. "Let me just stick it here. And if you think it's wrecked I can make another one. I'm not going anywhere."

Wyatt smiled at this, and she pressed the paper onto the nail, making a small hole in the top of the drawing. She liked the look of it, rustic on the wood plank.

She walked past him and lay down on the pile of blankets and pillows he now kept there just for this reason. Wyatt lay next to her and took her in his arms. "I really do love you, Sam."

Sam rolled on top of him. "I love you too. No question." She kissed him and luxuriated in the feel of the full length of her body on his. She pulled off his shirt and then hers. She was still in her bikini and watched his face as he slowly pulled on the red string around her neck and then the one at her back. She tossed it away and then bent down to him, letting the feeling of her bare chest on his move throughout her body. He kissed her, and she shivered.

He ran his fingers along her spine.

"Tell me again," she said into his neck.

"I love you."

"Tell me all the time, okay?"

"Promise," he said. He kissed her again and moved on top of her. He ran his hands down the sides of her body. She immediately wrapped her legs around his to keep him there. She was astonished by how much she wanted this.

Sam looped her thumbs under the elastic of Wyatt's shorts and started to pull them down. He caught her hands in his and gathered them to his chest. "Sam, what are we doing here?"

"I want to," she said.

"Are you sure?"

"This is my surest thing."

Looking back, Sam could think of nothing more natural than the two of them losing their virginity that night. There was no pretense of experience. There was no awkwardness about the hopeful box of condoms he'd stashed in his guitar case. Wyatt was like the ocean, and her body knew exactly what to do. As they lay there afterward in the moonlight, Wyatt whispered, "Sam, I am," and she thought she knew what he meant.

21

Wyatt

Wyatt thought a lot about how happy he was. He'd thought about being happy before, but it was usually in retrospect. This state of being happy and knowing it right in the moment was fascinating to him. He was going to spend the rest of his life this way: happy, with Sam.

"I have a surprise," Wyatt said, waiting outside the library.

Sam threw her arms around him and kissed him, right there with Mrs. Barton looking out the window. "Tell me."

"I love you."

Sam laughed. "No. The surprise."

"I stopped and changed Mr. Cameron's flat tire on my way to work today, because I'm a local hero, obviously."

"I am not surprised." She kissed him again. "So?"

"He's given me his boat for the day. It's small, just a two-seater, but why would we need more seats? We're going to Starfish Beach."

Sam threw her arms around him again. "Can we go now?"

"Yep. I even brought lunch."

They set off from the Camerons' dock on the canal and rode out into the open ocean. They rode past the stretch of their own beach, where their homes looked so cozy together. The engine was too loud for them to hear each other talk, but he loved looking over and seeing Sam smile into the ocean air.

Starfish Beach was a small stretch of sand and dunes that you could only access by boat or on foot. Mr. Cameron had told him exactly how to get there and how to tie up the boat. Wyatt unpacked a blanket, towels, and a bag of sandwiches and helped Sam off the boat. "I love what you've done with your hair."

She laughed and nudged him and tried to braid the whole mess.

They found the beach completely deserted. No one was using the picnic tables, but they decided to eat on the beach. They laid their towels on the sand and unwrapped their sandwiches.

"This is the nicest surprise I've ever had," Sam said, wiping mustard from her mouth.

"You are," he said.

"Have you always been so romantic? I don't remember this from when you were twelve."

"It's happened just recently," he said, and pulled her down to lie next to him. He closed his eyes and listened to the waves breaking just beyond the bluff. He felt the weight of Sam's head resting on his chest.

"How long do you think this will last?" she asked.

"What kind of a question is that?"

"I don't know." She was running her hand from his chest to his stomach in perfect rhythm with the waves. "I mean I can't imagine not being like this. Like, I don't want to go back."

Wyatt moved her hair out of her face so he could look at her. "If you've loved someone your whole life, it kind of makes sense that you'd love them forever."

NOW

22

I am parked in front of the Old Sloop Inn. Jack is in the passenger seat. These are the only things I know for sure. Because I must have imagined—hallucinated even—Jack's telling me that my dad has invited Wyatt to cruise to Starfish Beach with my family tonight. There is no way.

"Sam. It's no big deal. Your dad just wanted to thank him for fixing his car." My hands feel clammy against the steering wheel, but I don't want to let go. I am clearly not steering anything anymore.

"So all of us, my family and Wyatt, are cruising to Starfish Beach tonight? Were they going to tell me?" I flash on Wyatt and me, lying on Starfish Beach, talking about forever. I was stuck on that after we broke up, trying to reconcile Wyatt's saying he thought he'd love me forever and then his not, in fact, loving me forever. Dr. Judy helped me understand that when you're eighteen, you change your mind. Obviously. But I cannot walk through that space with Wyatt there.

"I just told you. It'll be fine. By the end of the night, things will be so normal. We're grown-ups, Sam. And so is he."

I rest my head on the steering wheel. We should have gone back to the city when we had the chance. I cannot explain what happened between Wyatt and me on that beach, because I know it will come out heavy.

He looks up at the inn. "Honestly, this place is a little tired, and all the nautical stuff isn't really my thing. But let's look. It's fun to see your mom so excited."

I want to start feeling excited.

23

My dad frequently borrows Harold Meyer's boat. In return, he does Harold's hedges. We drive to his house on the canal and get ready for our sunset outing. The boat seats eight, which was fine when we were my crew of nine, but now that Wyatt is coming, it's going to be way too tight. Wyatt arrives with Travis and Hugh. Granny hugs Wyatt, tight. Gracie throws herself at Wyatt, who picks her up and swings her around. *How long has this been going on?* I wonder. My dad loads two large coolers on board. Travis and Hugh are laden with champagne and plastic cups for the boat ride, and Jack hops off the boat to help them. It's too much, the weight of it. I worry the boat can't hold it all.

The ride to Starfish Beach is twenty minutes, but my dad's cruising slow enough for us to get through the champagne. Of course, we could have driven to any number of other beaches for a picnic, but my dad has no respect for efficiency. Granny Annie's face is in rapture as it's hit by the salt air. My mom has a scarf over her head, and I wish I'd thought to do the same. Honestly, I just wish we'd driven to

a restaurant. We'd be there by now and my hair would be
normal. I never go anywhere without a hair tie, and I am
slightly stunned that I've chosen today to let this happen.
As the wake sprays a delicious mist on my arms, my fingers
want to braid, but I won't allow it. Jack keeps his arm
around me as I hold my hair in a ponytail. I think Wyatt is
watching us, but I don't dare look.

We pull up to the dock and my dad kills the engine. The
silence fills my ears. For a split second I look at the players
on this stage, smiling and windswept, and nothing makes
sense. We climb out of the boat and I watch Travis and Wyatt walk down the dock together. Jack wheels both coolers
behind him, and I take Gracie's hand for reassurance.

The picnic tables are right on the beach, and we push
two together to accommodate our crew. My mom lays out
pink and white tablecloths and plastic plates and cups. She
scatters baguettes, cheese, and mounds of prosciutto along
the center of the table. When we're seated, my dad pours
rosé. "To the bride and her bridegroom!" he says. And we
all clink glasses.

Dinner is cold fried chicken and grilled vegetables, and
everything feels surprisingly easy. Wyatt and I are on opposite sides of the long table, separated lengthwise by four
bodies.

"So what about you two?" Wyatt asks Travis and Hugh.
"Any wedding plans?"

"Sort of," Travis says.

"Well, we would," says Hugh, "but it's not really a good
idea tax-wise." Travis rolls his eyes.

"More like it's Hugh's worst nightmare to have that

many people in a room looking at him," says Travis. "He wants to elope; I want a little hoopla. So we don't get married." He puts his arm around Hugh's chair in a way that makes me know they'll figure this out. I can't imagine either of them with anyone else.

"Ah, romance!" My mother laughs. "What about you, Wyatt? Anyone special out in Los Angeles?" What the heck? I don't want to know this. I look down at my food and am super-intensely aware of the fact that no one else is uncomfortable but me. I am living in a decade past where my mother wouldn't have dared mention Wyatt's name, much less casually ask if he had a girlfriend. I feel a flush of embarrassment at my own thoughts. I want to be a person who has moved on so completely that she's only mildly interested in the answer to this question. I look up and try to organize my features into neutral. I tilt my head the way dogs do, for good measure.

"Well, 'special' is a strong word," he says. "I've dated a singer on and off. Nothing serious." Wyatt looks satisfied that he's completely answered her question and bites into a chicken leg.

Granny is looking at me like I'm liquid in a beaker and she doesn't know what color I'm going to turn. I sip my wine.

"Where does she sing?" asks Jack. It's a good question. A great question. One that totally follows the thread of this conversation.

Wyatt is wiping his hands and is considering his answer for longer than I think the question warrants. Unless she sings in prison, this is a pretty straightforward question.

"Wherever she gets a gig," he says. "She's good."

"And you write songs?" My voice is small, like it's testing itself out after a long hiatus.

"Yes. And tinker around with cars. Which is how I got this dinner invitation." He raises his glass to my dad, and this line of questioning is over.

24

The next morning, I bike to town as soon as Jack leaves for the gym. It's Tuesday and I'm pretty sure I told my mother we would leave Wednesday. Jack insists I said Thursday, which I can't imagine I did. Pedaling my bike, I feel like I'm going for ice cream, but I really need a coffee. I've already had coffee, of course, but I don't feel like reading and I don't feel like staring at the ocean and watching my life story replay behind my eyes.

As soon as I round the corner onto Main Street, I realize that the highlight reel is still playing. The town of my childhood has not been so much as painted since I've been gone. The library where Wyatt stood and waited; Chippy's Diner, where we had a regular table and always shared fries; the ice-cream shop; Ginnie's Bakery. I stop in front of Chippy's and lock up my bike on the bike rack. The bike rack in front of which Wyatt ran his hands over my bare back and told me I was beautiful. I really need some coffee.

"Sam!" says Chippy as soon as I walk in. "To what do we owe the pleasure?"

"Hi!" Chippy has lost all of his hair and none of his charm. "I'd just like a coffee please. To go."

Chippy's smiling over my shoulder, and I know without turning around. "Hey there, Wyatt," he says.

I look down at my ten-dollar bill and pretend I haven't heard. Which is the only way I could have made this more awkward than it already was.

"Hey, Sam," Wyatt says, positioning himself next to me at the counter. "That was fun last night."

"Yeah. Thanks for fixing my dad's car." I force myself to turn toward him and look him in the eye. He hasn't shaved and has the faintest shadow along his jaw. This is different, and I can't look away from it. My hand wants to reach up and see what that feels like, Wyatt all grown up.

"Sure." He turns back to Chippy. "Can I have a coffee too please?"

Standing that close and looking right at Wyatt makes me feel like I am stuck in quicksand. I don't know how to be casual with him, like he's just a regular person. I turn back toward Chippy, and Wyatt and I wait in silence. I steal a glance at his hands, which are resting on the counter, and they are the same. Maybe a little sun-worn, but basically the same. I think there is something I should say to Wyatt, like there's an innocuous question I should ask, but my mind has gone blank, and it's becoming evident that not saying anything is more awkward than the awkward thing I might have said.

It takes forever to make these coffees. Chippy starts to fill my cup and the percolator is empty. He grinds more beans, empties and refills the filter, and sets it to brew. We can't walk away because we've ordered them, so we stand there, waiting. When Chippy has finally filled our paper cups and we are almost free to go, he hands them to us and goes into the kitchen to hunt for lids. We are marooned.

"Jack seems like a nice person," Wyatt says, finally. He reaches for the pitcher and pours milk in his coffee.

"Yes." I should be filling the air with words about what a nice person Jack is, but I am distracted by Wyatt's coffee.

"Do you want a sip or something?" he asks.

"No, it's just that I thought you drank your coffee black."

Wyatt takes a sip and turns to face me. "Why would you think that? You've never seen me drink coffee."

"That's not true."

"I started drinking coffee when I was twenty-five, and I am a hundred percent sure I haven't seen you since I was seventeen."

Is that true? Of course it is. When we were teenagers, I drank coffee and he didn't. He used to kiss me after I had coffee and say I smelled like an old man. And then he'd kiss me again anyway. Why is it that every time I imagined Wyatt drinking coffee, it was black like mine? Why is it that I've ever imagined Wyatt drinking coffee? I am on the precipice of mortified.

I shake my head. "I must have been thinking of someone else."

This wounds him a little; I can see it in the set of his mouth. It would wound me too if Wyatt confused anything about me with someone else.

Chippy comes back with our lids and we secure them. I hope we are putting the lid on this whole conversation.

"You biking back?" he says.

"Yeah," I say.

We walk outside and both head to the bike rack. He grabs his, and I kneel down to unlock mine.

"Expecting a crime wave?" he says.

"You never know," I say. I could fill a book with the words I don't say about the importance of protecting things that matter. Predictable outcomes.

A man who looks like a young Willie Nelson stops to say hello to Wyatt. "I was just down at the Owl Barn. The place is looking great."

"Yeah, I stopped by yesterday, I think we're in good shape," says Wyatt.

"Thanks so much for doing this, man."

"Are you kidding? It's fun to have it here," says Wyatt. "Sorry, Jason, this is Sam."

Jason shakes my hand and gives me a big smile. "Sam, like the song!"

"What song?" I ask.

He rolls his eyes in a good-hearted way. "'Sam, I Am,' of course. Good to see you, buddy." And he walks off.

"I should get back," I say to the sidewalk. It's so dumb that the mention of that nickname and that song makes me feel flustered. I steady my bike and, for the first time, consider how different biking with a cup of hot coffee is from biking with an ice-cream cone. The lid's on tight but there's plenty of opportunity for coffee to spill out of the sipping hole and scald me. Wyatt's standing there watching me, and there's no way to make a graceful exit on this bike. I hold up my coffee to him in a gesture meaning cheers, goodbye, and I give up. "This was a terrible idea," I say, and he laughs. I start to walk my bike home. I'm not getting burned again.

25

"He's really part of the family, isn't he?" Jack says with an eye-roll. Wyatt and Travis are walking up the beach late that afternoon, surfboards under their arms.

"He and Travis were friends when they were kids. They've been out of touch for a long time, this is kind of new," I say.

They walk through the dunes and leave their surfboards at the bottom of the porch steps. *Wyatt should be wearing a shirt,* I think. It's not right for him to be standing there, tan and wet and a little sandy. There's a tiny piece of seaweed on his shoulder, and my hand prickles with the desire to reach over and pick it off. The urge is so strong that I shove my hands in my armpits. This, I realize, is sort of a gross thing to do, and now I don't know what to do with my hands. *This is just the beach,* I think. *In the city, my body totally behaves itself.*

"You should have a shirt on," Jack is saying. I couldn't agree more, but *what*? "All your sunscreen will have washed off in the water and your shoulders are already red."

Wyatt looks at his shoulder and picks off the seaweed. "I've got to get better about that." He grabs a towel off a lounge chair and drapes it over his shoulders. He tosses another one to Travis. I am relieved.

"So, you helped bring the music festival to town?" I am trying for something in the category "Things a Friend Might Say."

"Yes," Wyatt says. "I know some of the people who recruit the bands."

"Are you going to go? I heard you play this morning, you sounded good." I am so awkward saying this, as if paying Wyatt a compliment is going to make me go up in flames.

Travis gets up from his lounge chair. "I'm going to need a beer for this." He walks into the house.

"Thanks." Wyatt smiles.

"So will you go?" I ask.

"Yeah, I'll stop by a few of the events. To see how it all turned out."

"This is how it happens," Jack says. "Connections. Good for you."

Travis is back with beers for just Wyatt and him. I ask, "So why did they decide to move the festival here?" Easy words, neutral conversation. I can totally do this.

"They didn't really want to try anything new, but I pitched it to them anyway. The quaint small town, easy access from the city. Newport is hard to get to and expensive." Wyatt sits down in a chair opposite us and his towel falls from his shoulders. Jack and I both stare nervously at those shoulders and Jack tosses him a bottle of sunscreen. Wyatt grabs his T-shirt instead and pulls it over his head. It's his old Chicago Cubs T-shirt, which has now been washed within an inch of its life. It is paper-thin with a small rip along the neck where his left collarbone is exposed. He might as well be sitting there completely naked. I blink the image away.

Wyatt goes on. "I think what sold them was the fact that Skip Warren got married here. At the Old Sloop Inn actually. The guy in charge is a huge tennis fan, so that sort of legitimized the place."

Jack leans forward in his chaise. "Skip Warren got married here?" And to me, "Did you know this?"

"I guess. We were kids, I think," I say.

"You were fifteen," Wyatt says, and smiles at me the tiniest bit.

"I can't believe I didn't know that. I mean, Skip Warren. He's the whole reason I started playing tennis." I don't really have it in me to debunk this statement, but the whole reason Jack started playing tennis is that his whole family has played tennis since they were able to walk.

Travis raises his beer to Jack. "Well here's to the Old Sloop Inn."

26

"Absolutely not." I can't remember when I've been so emphatic with Jack. We're in the garage apartment, which was my idea because I absolutely need to have sex with him to get my head back on straight. I need a fresh, successful sexual experience to wash the image of Wyatt in that T-shirt from my mind. Jack's ruined the moment by telling me his parents want to visit tomorrow.

"Why not? They think it sounds like a nice place for the wedding, and they love the whole Skip Warren thing."

"Skip Warren? Are there real people who care about Skip Warren?" I'm sitting on the nicely made bed while Jack carefully unbuttons his shirt like this is actually going to happen.

He stops halfway down. "I am one of those people. Plus my parents make three. Look, let them come for the day. We'll see them for a walk around and dinner, that's it."

It's too much. I put my head in my hands and try to think of something to say that will make Jack know how I feel. "It's too much."

"Wherever we get married, we're going to have all of our family together. This is a mini version of it. And if they like it, maybe we will get married out here. Maybe everyone will be happy."

Jack's mom, Donna, is an office manager. She's precise like Jack, and I have to guess that the books where she works are balanced and dust free. I love precise people; I'm marrying one, after all. I like the way she sends me a birthday card that arrives exactly the day before my birthday each year. I bet she renews her driver's license online before it expires. Like Jack, she has a standing hair appointment to keep the edges razor sharp. People like this don't blow up their families. People like this have long-term-care insurance and living wills.

My parents have met Jack's twice in four years. Both times we met for dinner in the city, neutral territory. Jack's dad, Glen, won my dad over with questions about a *New York Times* article he'd read about *Current*. Donna won my mom over by saying that I'm the daughter she's always dreamed of. They are truly lovely people.

"Okay, fine," I say.

"Good," Jack says, pulling down the covers for me. "Because they'll be here in the morning."

I'm thrown by this, both the fact that they're coming and the fact that it was a done deal before I even knew about it. I'm thrown by the prospect of Donna walking into my mother's kitchen. But I look up at Jack, who is opening himself up to Oak Shore and my family, and I start to undress.

27

So much for leaving on Wednesday. Jack's parents are arriving at noon, and I think I hear Jack tell my dad that we're staying through the weekend. This can't be right. Jack leaves for a morning at the gym, and Gracie challenges me to swim all the way down to the cove. We walk down to the water, and worries chase each other around in my head— the state of my job, what Jack's parents are going to think of Mom's driftwood collection, the possibility of running into Wyatt again when I'm half-dressed. The cold water tickles my feet and soon I am swimming alongside Gracie. The knots start to untangle. As I get into a rhythm and my stroke clicks in, I see things from a different perspective. I recognize it as the braver, lighter perspective of a younger me. I think about my job and how much I've learned there. If I'm fired, I have the skills to find another one. Maybe even one where there's room for new ideas. I picture my mother making paper and think how impressed Donna might be by that. How many people know how to make paper? My what-ifs have lost their heaviness.

When we get to the cove, I am shocked by the beauty of the linden tree. I haven't been down here in years, and it's the same, if bent slightly more by the wind.

"I can't believe you swam that far," says Gracie.

"I know. I wasn't thinking about it, I just kept going." I'm out of breath, but I like the way my body feels. We sit down at the base of the tree, side by side, with all the shells scattered in front of us.

"You seem happier," says Gracie. She's making a circle in the sand with her index finger.

"Happier than what?"

"Than in the city. Happier than when you're dressed in stiff clothes. I don't know why you're so weird about coming to the beach."

I put my arm around her. I do know why, but she doesn't need to hear it. "It sounds like Jack wants to stay the rest of the week," I say. "Can we do this again tomorrow morning?"

Gracie smiles at me like she hasn't seen me for a long time.

JACK AND I meet Donna and Glen at the Old Sloop Inn for lunch. I was relieved when my parents decided to stay home and get things organized for dinner on the back porch. I almost asked my mom to put her papermaking operation away and move the seaweed into Dad's studio, but the sight of her puttering around her chaotic kitchen and humming softly to herself gave me pause. My mother is so happy and complete in the world she's created. I am sometimes so uncomfortable in mine. I envy her this and decided not to say anything. *How many people know how to make paper?*

"This is so exciting!" Donna says, giving me a tight hug. "Skip Warren. I had no idea." This confuses me a bit, because I was sure she was about to say our wedding was the exciting thing.

"I can't believe it either," says Jack. "And don't you love this place?"

We walk through the small lobby into the main dining room, where the wedding would be. It really is charming, with whitewashed wood and lighting fixtures secured by nautical rope. It has a beachy elegance to it that I like, I guess the next best thing to having the whole thing outside.

"It's great," says Glen. "Let's see about the food." Then to me, "Your parents are all for this place, right?"

This Old Sloop Inn thing seems to be getting away from me. If I throw my parents in as a yes, this will feel like a done deal. "They just want whatever we want." We sit at our table, and Donna and Jack carefully unfold their napkins and spread them on their laps.

"Donna and I drove by Warren Woods on our way into town," Glen says. "Gorgeous park. Perfect place for a rehearsal dinner."

"That's a great idea. The whole wedding weekend will have kind of a low-key theme," Jack says. I'm sure I've misheard him because there's no way I'm having a Washed-Up Tennis Player–themed wedding.

"It's a great park," I say. "Travis used to play baseball

there in the summertime. But Jack doesn't want to plan anything outdoors in October."

"Well, no, there I would. It probably won't rain."

"And we'd have a plan B for sure," says Donna. "I have the perfect caterer, and they work with a rental company who will bring in everything we need."

The three of them are nodding and smiling like we've just discovered a new clean energy source. I can't think of any reason to disagree with them. My parents are going to be ecstatic.

"THE WASHED-UP TENNIS player?" my dad asks over dinner. He's barbecued chicken and my mom has made orzo and a chopped salad. The table looks beautiful, and I am ashamed of myself for dreading this moment. My parents are gracious and happy, and this shared enthusiasm for my wedding gives everyone tons to talk about.

"He was a cad," Gramps says. "Slept with every girl on Long Island before he knocked one up and had to marry her."

"Dad," my mom laughs. "That's not true."

"As true as I'm sitting here."

"Well, this isn't to do with them," Donna says. "It's a beautiful historic park, and the inn is just perfect."

"I say we book it," says my dad.

Jack looks at me, and I shrug. I'm not shrugging *I don't know*, I think I'm shrugging *What difference does it make?* I can't quite picture what this wedding is going to feel like, and at this point, Long Island and Connecticut seem interchangeable.

Donna gives me a smile. "Let's leave it to the bride. You let us know what you decide." She raises her glass and says, "To the bride!"

I am waiting to feel one way or another. I check my stomach for a hooray or an absolutely not. There's nothing there but acceptance and a bit of relief that this decision is close to being made. I have let go, and this wedding is probably going to be the one thing I insisted it not be: on Long Island. I don't really mind.

After blueberry pie, we walk Donna and Glen around the porch to their car. It's a black Mercedes sports car of some sort, making me suspect Glen had a midlife crisis in the past few years.

"Oh hey." Wyatt waves from his driveway. He's in jeans and a T-shirt, holding his guitar case. If he weren't about to get into his mother's station wagon, he'd look like he stepped off an album cover.

"That's Wyatt," I say, like it's a confession.

"Hello," Glen and Donna say.

Wyatt walks over and shakes their hands. "That's a beautiful car," he says.

"Thank you. Gets me from point A to point B," Glen says with a laugh.

"Nice way to travel," Wyatt says.

"He's a mechanic," says Jack. "At a Shell station. In Los Angeles." And it's not nice. I don't know why, but there's a tone to it.

"Not exactly, but I'm off duty tonight," says Wyatt, like the punch didn't even land. "I'm headed over to the Owl Barn to help some of the bands warm up." He raises his guitar case.

"Oh, are you a performer?" asks Donna, with her hand over her heart like it just fluttered. I swear if I didn't know her, I'd think she was flirting.

"I mostly just write songs." He gives her a genuinely kind smile, like he's glad she asked. Like he's completely at peace. I like knowing this about his life in LA, that he's still working at it even if he's not going to perform. "Well, it was nice meeting you. Your son's made a great choice."

"We know. We couldn't be happier. And it looks like they might decide to get married out here," Donna says.

Wyatt looks at me in surprise.

"It was the draw of Skip Warren," I tell him.

He laughs, "Of course. Your favorite."

28

It's Thursday, and I can't believe I've stayed here for nearly a week. I also can't believe I am starting to come around to the idea of having my wedding out here. I imagine my friends from the city coming out and seeing this other part of me, suntanned and easy. I don't know where I've been keeping her, this other Sam, but I want to think they'd like her.

I'm up early. I've slept with the windows open, and I can hear the waves crashing. I lie in bed and let the sound wash over me again and again. I can feel the chill of water on my skin and imagine myself swimming all the way down to the linden tree. I hear the water rush by my ears and feel the way my shoulders would stretch with each stroke. I get up and put on my bathing suit immediately, the way I would have done as a kid, just knowing that the ocean was going to be woven into my day.

Out on the deck, the morning is breathtaking. There's a slight breeze coming off the water that blows the dunes gracefully to the left. Gulls are gliding overhead, stretching their wings to embrace the day. I hear a few notes coming from the treehouse. Wyatt is up. I imagine myself walking off the porch and into his yard and climbing up the rope ladder. I'd say, "Hey." And he'd say, "Hey, Sam-I-am." He'd smile at me in that way that had made me feel whole and seen my entire life. And maybe that would be it, we'd be friends.

Wyatt is playing a song that sounds a little bit like "Sam, I Am," but different. I love that song, of course. It was Missy McGee's first big hit and was the number one song on the radio forever. The first time I heard it, I was a junior at NYU. I was in a bar and thought I was hallucinating. I shushed the hair-gelled guy I was talking to so I could hear the chorus. Everything about it reminded me of Wyatt. The lyrics about catching the breath of the person you're in love with and the rhythm of the music put me right back in the treehouse. For about six months there was no escaping that song at every party. If I heard it in a bar, I would walk outside; if I heard it in the car, I would change the station. If I was alone with Gracie, I would let myself listen.

Years ago I read an article about Missy McGee in *People* where she was talking about old relationships gone wrong. And I thought, *One of those guys must be the Sam in her song. And she must have felt all the same things about him that Wyatt and I felt about each other.* I realized that everyone who's young and in love must feel exactly the same. In a weird way, it made me feel better.

Which I guess is why it was such a relief when I met Jack. I love Jack, but I don't need to be touching him all the time. There isn't this feeling of holding on so tightly because I might fall into the abyss if I let go. There has never been a moment where I felt like he was a part of me; he is just right next to me, a partner. Love like this is so much more manageable, so much less terrifying. He has his work and his friends, and so do I. He has wonderful parents. Sometimes we visit them together. Sometimes Jack goes alone, and I enjoy a weekend in the apartment by myself, or with Gracie, not talking about exercising. This kind of side-by-side love feels like a manageable kind of joy. I now understand that this is what grown-up love is. It's not that the thing with Wyatt was magic and this isn't; it's just that back then I was sixteen years old. I hate it when Dr. Judy is right.

When I met Jack in the back of that cab for the first time, I thought, *I want this.* The thought grew louder in my head as I took him in. His shoulders and his haircut made him seem in control, as if he as a person was impervious to an unexpected gust of wind. He wore a waxed Barbour jacket, warm but also ready for rain. He turned his body toward me as we drove uptown in a way that made me feel like he was interested in me too.

He was going to Thirty-Fourth Street, and as we got closer, it didn't look like he was going to ask for my number. In a panic, I started leaving him bread crumbs in case he decided he wanted to track me down later.

"I work for Human Corps on Forty-Third Street," I said. He could wait outside the office and ask me out. Maybe there would be flowers.

Then, "It's human resources consulting. My Twitter handle is Saminhr, but no one gets it and they spell out 'salmon' like I'm a fish. There's no such thing as salmon HR. I mean they all swim the way they're supposed to, right?" This was not my finest attempt at the art of conversation, but we were half a block from where he was getting out. *I want this.*

When we pulled up in front of his office, he handed me a ten-dollar bill and said, "Well, Sam in HR, it was nice meeting you. Have a good day." He lingered for a second but then shut the door and crossed the street.

Two days later, he sent me a Twitter message inviting me out for sushi. It was a Tuesday and he arrived at the restaurant with slightly wet hair. I now know this would have been a result of his post-tennis shower.

I want this, I thought.

WYATT PLAYS A song I've never heard straight through without stopping. It's good and I wonder what words he'd put with it. He starts on another song, effortless and unhalting, and I think I know this one. I wonder if he's singing quietly along or if he's given up singing altogether. In my head, I can hear his slightly tentative voice.

I sort of hope he settles down with someone. It would be nice for both of us to have ended up with real, stable partners. When I think of all the shattered pieces of his life, all shattered at once, I sort of understand why he walked away. Plus, I got Gracie out of this whole thing. He got nothing.

"You're up early," my mom says, joining me with Granny and three cups of coffee. She tilts her head toward the music. "Nice thing to wake up to." It was the wrong thing to say. I feel the innuendo in my gut; she must see it on my face. "I just mean the music." Granny stifles a laugh.

"I know. It's just so disorienting. I feel like I've walked into an old photo album. How is it possible that he's here and he's exactly the same, doing all the same things?"

"He's not exactly the same. Just because he's wearing the same clothes and playing the same guitar doesn't mean he hasn't grown up," my mom says.

"I guess."

"And it really has been a long time. Maybe you two could be friends."

"No chance," says Granny.

I give her an eye-roll. "Of course we could be friends."

"So what are we going to do about this singer he's seeing?" Granny asks.

"Nothing. Because I'm getting married, remember?"

"That's right," says Granny, like I've jogged her memory. "That Jack is awfully handsome, might get on my nerves after a while." My mom and I laugh because that's just so Granny. She's suspicious of shiny things.

Wyatt stops playing, and we look out at the water. "I adore Jack," my mom says. Here we go. "But I think you should try to talk things through with Wyatt before you get married, put the whole thing behind you so he's not some kind of fantasy lurking in your head. Jack is the sort of man I've dreamed of you marrying, but you don't want to start a marriage with any doubts."

"Did you?"

"No, not a single one. From our third date, I thought I'd die if I didn't marry your dad."

Granny leans in. "She was obsessed."

"I was," my mom says. "And that's not always a healthy kind of love."

"I say it's the only kind," says Granny.

My mom smiles at Granny. "Maybe," she says. What she doesn't say is that it's dangerous and can completely destroy you. What she doesn't say is that she would throw her body into a raging fire before ever seeing me hurt again.

"Never forget that I can see inside your head," she says, and actually pokes my nose like I'm six. "There's a little flicker there that I find mildly disturbing. For sure you should marry Jack, but clear the air with Wyatt first."

"There's no flicker."

"Oh, there's a flicker all right," Granny laughs. I really can't stand these two right now.

THEN

29

Sam

"Anybody want to swim down to the cove for sunset?" asked Sam. There were ten of them on the beach, including Travis and Michael.

"It's too far," said Travis. "I'm worn out already."

"We'll take breaks," Sam said.

"Don't believe her," said Wyatt. "She doesn't take breaks."

Sam looked up at the sky. "We only have about twenty minutes. Who's in?" Sam was on her feet and could already feel the pull of the ocean. She could feel the cool water on her skin and hear the muffled sound of her own strokes. Wyatt was the only one who stood up.

"All right, Sam, but we're walking back. I swear you're going to break me."

Sam smiled and ran into the ocean. As she started to swim, she lost track of Wyatt. She didn't know if he was ahead of her or behind her, but she knew he was there. She tried to push the recurring thought away—in a few weeks he would be back in Illinois for his senior year. She'd be back in the city with friends who could never appreciate how completely she'd been transformed. She'd take the ACT, she'd finish junior year. And it would be summer again. She could do this, she thought, arms cutting through the water. Wyatt had said forever.

When they got to the cove, Wyatt took her hand and led her up the shore. She shook out her hair and tied it in a knot on top of her head.

"Seriously, Sam, you're going to kill me." Wyatt was still catching his breath as they walked hand in hand toward the linden tree.

Sam surveyed her old collection of shells. Some were half covered in sand, and she dusted them off. The sun was setting and she could feel Wyatt watching her.

She looked up. "What?"

Wyatt shrugged. "I was just thinking this would be a nice place to get married."

Sam looked out on the beach in front of the tree. The sun was starting to set, just the beginning yellow-to-orange stage. "To who?" she asked, stepping toward him.

"I don't know. I'll find somebody." He put his arms around her still-wet back and kissed her. Before she knew it their bathing suits were in the sand and they were wrapped up in each other right under that tree. She looked up at the dark green leaves and had two thoughts before she gave in to the bliss of Wyatt touching every part of her body: *Summer is almost over* and *This is exactly where I'm going to get married.*

30

Wyatt

Most nights, all the kids would meet on the beach as soon as it was dark. Sometimes they went to someone's house, but in late August time was running out, and no one wanted to waste it being inside. When everyone was seated around the fire, Wyatt saw their faces at every age. They'd been little kids sneaking over to the older kids' bonfire, they'd been thirteen, fourteen, and he'd been falling in love with Sam all along. He felt like he and Sam had always been on this stretch of sand, and he loved that they'd be there again at the same time next summer.

Wyatt wished he had his guitar, as the sound of everyone talking, mixed with the breeze coming off the ocean and the crackling of the fire, brought a tune into his mind. There was a sound to summer music, he thought. It sounded like warm air.

He wanted to be a person who could just pick up a guitar and play for people without worrying that it was no good. The stakes were pretty low with this crew, and with Sam sitting next to him, her legs draped over his, he felt more confident than he ever had. But his music was such a big, aching dream that he wasn't ready to risk having an audience of more than one.

"I hate the end of summer," Sam said to everyone.

"I don't know how you two are going to survive without each other," said Travis. Everyone kind of laughed, and Wyatt tried to keep the pain off his face. This was something they were trying not to talk about, how they were going to manage an entire nine months apart. They'd spend next summer at the beach, then he'd head out to LA. Sam would be a senior then and would apply to USC and UCLA. They never really covered more than the broad strokes of how that life was going to fall into place. Instead, they talked about what their view would look like, how strange the beach would look facing the wrong way.

"It's going to suck," said Sam, because the time apart was going to suck. He put his arm around her and pulled her in tight. Holding her close, he could feel the ache of not being able to touch her for so long. Everything had a flip side.

Sam unwrapped herself from his arms and stood up. "Anyone want to play Capture the Flag? Just one last time?"

31

Sam

It was almost Labor Day, and summer felt like the last inch of water draining from the bathtub. Wyatt met Sam at the library and took her out to lunch at the diner. "It's payday, m'lady," he said.

When they'd ordered turkey sandwiches and fries to share, Sam said, "So, I had the talk with my dad last night."

Wyatt's eyes went huge. "What do you mean 'talk'?"

Sam smiled. "Like about you and me."

"Oh my God, is he going to kill me? I'll totally marry you right now if you want."

Sam laughed. "No, he was really cute about it. He just came in and sat on my bed and was like, 'Sammy, seems like you're having a pretty big love affair this summer.' And I was like, 'Yeah.'"

"Is he going to kill me or not?"

"No, it was nothing like that. He said he was happy for me. That there's nothing more exciting in life than that pull toward another person. It was really nice. And it made me feel happy for my parents, that he feels that way."

Wyatt's whole body relaxed. "He's so cool. Your whole family is so cool. Everything just right out in the open so there are no land mines to step on."

"Is it any better with your parents?"

"It's worse, I think. Michael's wasted most of the time and they don't say a word about it. They know for sure that I'm not going to college, but we don't talk about what I am doing. It's just this big, thick silence in the house." Wyatt peeled the label off his bottle of Coke. "I wish my dad would be like, 'Oh hey, son, I see you're in love.' Or even 'Oh hey, I see you're' *anything*."

Sam said, "Yeah, I guess we're talkers."

"It's awesome," he said. "Your family is the best."

32

Wyatt

On the Saturday night before Labor Day, the Holloways and the Popes were hosting a party on the beach. Every family on Saltaire Lane was invited. They had tables set in the sand and a buffet of shrimp, fried chicken, and potato salad. There were big buckets with iced wine and beer, and Sam wore a short white sundress. Those are the parts Wyatt would remember the most clearly before it all happened. The crunch of the shrimp, the dill in the potato salad, the feel of Sam's dress when his hand rested on her waist.

Laurel was gathering up the empty glass water bottles, struggling with four of them in her hands. They were out of water, and she must have noticed that people were getting a bit tipsy. Wyatt made his way over to her and took the bottles. "Let me," he said. "Need anything else from inside?"

Laurel smiled her gratitude. "No, but thank you. I'm exhausted."

Wyatt made his way up the beach, to the path in the dunes, two empty bottles in each hand. He'd fully intended to fill the bottles at the Holloways' house—they had a water cooler in the kitchen—but he was hot and he knew the water from the dispenser in the door of his refrigerator would be ice-cold. *The only thing that's better at my house,* he'd remember thinking. If it hadn't been so hot, he probably would have filled up the bottles at Sam's house. It was faster, and they were Sam's bottles. If it hadn't been so hot, maybe nothing would have changed.

He passed the pool, opened the sliding glass door, and heard it, a muffled gasp. He switched on the light and tried to make sense of his mother sitting on the kitchen counter with her arms around Bill Holloway's neck.

"Mom?" he heard himself say.

"Wyatt. Oh, we were just . . ." He didn't stay for the rest.

He ran out to the treehouse and texted Sam that he wasn't feeling well and was going to bed. Then he sat in his beach chair, motionless, watching the rest of the party. He saw his mother walk back out to the beach, rejoining the group. He wondered if this would be just one more thing that the Popes didn't talk about. Michael's drunk, Wyatt's not going to college, Mom's an adulterer. He watched Bill walk out moments later, looking around, presumably for him. Wyatt would have to tell Sam, but he didn't even know what to say.

He woke up on the floor of the treehouse to find Sam climbing under the blankets next to him. She curved her body right into his, the way she always did, and rested her head on his chest. "This is a weird place to sleep if you're not feeling well," she whispered.

"I'm okay," he said.

"Do you love me?" she asked, like she did so often. It was rhetorical at this point, a game.

"I do," he said, and pulled her closer. He ran the words through his head: *I have something to tell you.* Or, *I saw something.* She would be crushed, and honestly, he was too. It wasn't even so much his mother's doing something like that to his father. For all he knew, she couldn't stand him. He felt more let down by Bill, like the one thing in the world that he'd thought was perfect was not. And the thought of Sam's knowing what he knew was too much for him.

"You're quiet," she said, running her hand over his chest.

"I'm asleep," he said. "Stay with me." And she did.

WHEN THE SUN came up, Sam snuck down the rope ladder and back to her house. Wyatt woke hours later and found his dad and Bill sitting by the pool. Frank was leaning back, arms folded over his chest. Bill had his head in his hands. There was no way into the house without walking by them. "I'm sorry, son," said Bill, whose son he was not.

Wyatt just stood there.

"I didn't know if you'd tell your dad, but I didn't want that burden on you. This is my fault, mine and your mom's, I guess, and it's for me to carry, not you." *So goddamn perfect,* thought Wyatt. This guy was flawless, except for the obvious.

"Glad you feel better, then," said Wyatt, and walked into the house.

His mother was in the kitchen, wiping up spills that weren't there. "I did everything wrong," she said, not looking up.

Yes, he thought. *Everything.*

By noon, Frank was headed to the airport to fly back to Florida. Sam would be at work at the library, getting off in an hour. Wyatt took the truck and waited out front. When she saw him, her face opened up in a smile. She hopped in the car and kissed him. He kissed her extra, in case this was the last time.

"You'll be happy to know my parents are in a fight," she joked. "I heard them arguing when I left this morning, just like regular people."

"Sam."

"I'm joking, maybe it's not funny. But I sort of thought, *Wow, is this what regular parents do?*"

"Sam. I need to tell you. Something's happened."

They were still parked in front of the library on Main Street; the car was hot and the windows were down. Sam turned to him and took his hand.

"You're scaring me a little. What?"

Wyatt looked down at her hand in his, so angry at Bill for creating this moment.

"Last night I saw your dad and my mom, kind of making out. There's been some kind of an affair and my dad went back to Florida."

Sam just looked at him. "I don't understand."

"I know, this is really hard to hear, and it was really hard to see."

Sam turned away from him and stared straight out the windshield. The silence that followed put new space between them. Finally, Sam said, "Take me home."

When Wyatt pulled into his driveway, Sam went right into her house without saying a word. He tried to imagine what she'd find in there. Would Travis be home? Would they all just talk about it? Wyatt was overcome with jealousy at the thought. His dad had just gotten up and left, and the Holloways were probably already in group therapy. *Thanks, Bill, for blowing up my family.*

APPARENTLY, LAUREL COULDN'T spend another night next door to Marion. But, of course, she wasn't going to leave Bill alone living next to her. From his kitchen window, Wyatt could see Bill and Travis packing up the car to go back to Manhattan.

He texted Sam: What's happening? Are you leaving?

Sam: Looks like it. Can I come say goodbye?

Wyatt: Meet me at the beach

They had ten minutes to say everything that was hopefully going to make this thing okay. Wyatt sat with his arm around Sam and felt the weight of her legs draped over his. He felt her head on his shoulder, exactly where it was meant to be, and ran his fingers over the tangle of her hair. He wasn't sure that he'd processed what he'd seen last night or that he had any idea of what was going to happen, but he did know that right in his arms was everything that mattered. "I love you and this has nothing to do with us, okay?" he kept saying.

Sam cried and let him hold her. "I don't understand how this can be happening."

"I can't believe I'm not going to see you tomorrow." Wyatt felt emptied out as he said these words, as he imagined his body alone without Sam. He felt the happiness that he'd been so acutely aware of all summer start to melt away, and anger filled the empty space.

33

Sam

Sam wouldn't have been ready to say goodbye to Wyatt on Labor Day under normal circumstances, but now, saying goodbye like this, she felt like she'd had something ripped from her body. Something that was critical to her functioning. Her family was silent in the car, and as they got closer to Manhattan, Sam felt the panic you feel when you've become disoriented in the water and you don't remember which way is up. She felt like everything she'd thought she knew about the world had been wrong.

"MY PARENTS HAVE started therapy," she told Wyatt on the phone in late September.

"I cannot imagine your dad in therapy."

"Me neither. It's weird here, this thick tension in the apartment and my dad sort of walking on eggshells. I'm pretty sure my mom could get him to do anything she wanted right now." It was almost as if her mother was in a newly restructured marriage, and she was enjoying the position of power. It was unnerving.

"Well I hope she makes him suffer for a little while longer, he deserves it."

"Wyatt."

"I mean it. He broke my family; he can sweat it out for a little while before he gets his happy ending." Sam wanted to say that Bill hadn't broken their family, that Wyatt himself had told her a million times how broken it already was. But there was anger in his voice that Sam had never heard before. She was scared to push back.

"How's your dad doing?" she asked.

"I don't know. Looks like he's going to stay in Florida and my mom's going to keep the beach house. He's angry and quiet. So I guess nothing's new."

These conversations went on throughout the fall. Some days they caught up like old friends and then talked about how much they missed one another. On those days they talked about moving out to Los Angeles. Sam had a packed junior year course load and was studying for the ACT, her ticket to either UCLA or USC. Wyatt just wanted to graduate and get his life started. On other days it was tense, especially if Wyatt asked about her parents.

"They seem a little better," Sam said. It was November and the air in the apartment did feel lighter.

"So they go to a shrink a few times and suddenly your dad's not chasing women?"

Sam's chest went tight. She knew that making excuses for her dad just made Wyatt angrier, but she was coming around to accepting the whole thing, and if Wyatt could too, everything could go back to normal. "He says it was about his art, about being so desperate for a new idea that he lost his grip on reality."

Wyatt let out a hard breath. "Remind me never to use my music as an excuse to act like an asshole."

These exchanges were usually punctuated with "sorry" or "let's not do this," but their relationship was poisoned. It was impossible for Wyatt to think of his mom alone in that cold house without blaming Bill. He was constantly reacting to all the ways Sam was like her dad, even the things he used to say he loved about her, like her imagination and her directness. Sam could feel Wyatt closing off. Even the sound of his *I love you* lost its tenderness. He said it the way you'd say goodbye.

34

Wyatt

Wyatt couldn't have imagined how his family could possibly be more screwed up until his mother visited him at school to tell him that Michael had been thrown out of college for repeated drunk and disorderly conduct. He was relieved when she left. His dorm room was too small to hold his family's pain.

He sat on his bed, holding his guitar but not playing. He thought about Sam and how much he wished she were there with him. He wished the two of them could run away from their families and just go back to what they'd had. This was a peaceful thought, and he decided to call Sam while he had it, to make up for being so angry these past few weeks.

"Hey, Sam-I-am," he said when she picked up.

"You haven't called me that in a while. Is this the Wyatt I used to know?"

"I'm sorry, I've been such a jerk. I love you more than anything."

He heard her let out a breath. "I love you too."

Wyatt walked over to his window and pushed it open in hopes that a breeze or the sound of kids on the quad might wash away the ugliness that had enveloped his family. "So Michael got kicked out of school. Basically for being a drunk." His voice caught as he said it, and he squeezed his eyes shut. "My mom was just here to tell me."

"That's awful. I'm sorry."

"Yeah, no kidding. I guess it's just the last step in the total destruction of my family." He could hear the anger creep back into his voice. He felt incapable of controlling it.

"How's your mom?"

"She apologized a lot, like everything's her fault. Mostly for never talking about anything and for letting things get this bad. She seems broken." He stopped himself from saying *Your dad broke us.*

35

Sam

When, in April, Laurel announced she was pregnant, Sam knew her parents were going to stay together. Everything was different in their apartment. It was as if someone had thrown open the windows and relief had washed through the place. Without having taken her first breath, Gracie started to work her magic. Her parents were fine, and now there was going to be a baby.

Sam called Wyatt to tell him. "That's disgusting," he said.

"Well, yes, they're old, but it's kind of nice. Starting over."

"Yep. Your dad's a real ladies' man."

Sam was quiet on the phone while Wyatt's anger simmered. She hated hearing Frank's sharp sarcasm in his voice. She knew he just meant that it wasn't fair that her family was growing when his was slipping away. But she couldn't keep taking this.

"That wasn't fair, what you said about my dad."

"Nothing's really fair, Sam."

"If we're going to be okay, if we're going to go out to LA, be together, we need to get past this."

"'Get past this,'" he repeated. "For you it was a kiss in the kitchen, with a new baby to make it all better. For me, it was divorce, a dad I don't see, a mother living alone, and a brother who's totally screwed up his life. Everything is just so damn easy for the Holloways."

"Wyatt. Please." Sam was trying not to cry.

"You know what, maybe I'll head out to LA early, skip the summer in that hellhole. You can come whenever."

"You mean like in a year? Like I won't see you for a year?"

"Yeah, that sounds good. Enjoy the new baby and your happy family."

"Wyatt. Stop." She was crying now. "Please come for the summer. You've got to get past it."

"Oh, okay, let me get on that." The call disconnected and Sam felt herself slip away.

SAM SAT ON a bench in Washington Square Park staring at her phone. She hadn't heard from Wyatt in eleven days. It had been years since she'd gone a day without at least getting a text. She went to school most days but occasionally found herself derailed by her own feet and sitting on this bench until three p.m. She replayed the summer and the summer before that in her mind. She tried to remember what it felt like to laugh until your body shook or to follow a whim wherever it took you. She was currently having a hard time finding the energy to get up off this bench.

During these eleven days she had sent two texts that she was starting to hate herself for: Wyatt please, and This can't be happening. Sipping her coffee and watching his reply not pop up, she felt small and rigid, like one of the flat gray rocks on the beach that just washed out with the tide. She felt a total lack of agency, like her legs and her spirit had stopped collaborating to move her forward. Her body no longer knew what to do.

She found relief in the water. She swam at the YMCA in the evenings, letting the ice-cold water shock her skin into feeling a different kind of pain. She wanted to tell Wyatt that her stamina had improved, that there would be no more breaks when they swam to the cove. She imagined his dramatic groan over this fact, and she ached all over again. With each push off the wall, she welcomed the throbbing of her muscles. If she could swim a full mile, Wyatt would call. If Wyatt would call, she would sleep a full night. If she slept a full night, she would be Sam again.

She returned to the apartment deliberately too late for dinner. The swimming served the dual purpose of wearing her out and keeping her from facing her happy-ish, healing parents across the table. She took a plate into her room each night and continued to make deals with God. If she finished her art history paper in less than ninety minutes, Wyatt would call. As she typed and focused on the Renaissance, she felt the brief relief of feeling in control. She was going to make Wyatt appear. When she completed her task and her phone was quieter than ever, she lay in her bed, numb. She had to stop playing this game. Actually, if she could stop playing this game for a full week, then Wyatt would call. She was in a loop of deals with God.

If she got a few hours of sleep, she'd dig herself out of the darkness and lean toward happier thoughts. She clung to the fact that Wyatt wouldn't be able to keep this up if they saw each other in person. He loved her, she didn't have any doubt about that. Even though she no longer knew who her father was, she knew exactly what was in Wyatt's heart. He'd decide to come to the beach for the summer and everything would go back to normal. Senior year, USC acceptance, Venice Beach. All as planned.

Sam was telling herself this story on a Thursday afternoon as she let herself into the apartment. Laurel was on the phone in the kitchen and hurried to hang up when she saw her.

"What?" Sam asked.

"That was Travis. He heard from Michael that Wyatt's not coming to the beach after graduation."

Sam plopped down onto the couch and Laurel sat next to her, wrapping an arm around her shoulder. "Because of me?" Sam asked.

"Because of all of it. They're renting out the house, and he's going straight to Los Angeles."

"I don't mean to be dramatic," Sam said, "but I don't think I can handle this."

"Honey, I'm sure he's going to come around. His life has been turned upside down; maybe he just needs some time."

These were the right words to say, but Sam could see the fear on her mother's face. Laurel, recovering from her own heartbreak, couldn't bear seeing Sam suffer her own.

Sam went into her room and cried until she'd completely exhausted herself. She longed for crying yourself to sleep to be a real thing. Sleep would have been a break. But she felt like she was on high alert, abandoned in this weird space with a heart full of terrifying feelings.

It was dark when her dad came in with a cookie and a cup of tea. "I heard," he said, sitting down on the side of her bed. "I don't know how I'm ever going to make this up to you."

"I don't either," Sam said, and turned over.

"I was desperate, Sam. It was so selfish."

"It really was."

"You're going to have to forgive me sometime."

Sam turned to face him. "Actually, that's one thing I don't have to do."

36

Wyatt

Wyatt flew with his mom back to New York immediately after his high school graduation. It was too early for the Holloways to be there, as Sam would still be in school. He stayed one night before getting in his dad's old truck and driving across the country. As he made his way west, sleeping in the bed of the truck and occasionally splurging on a motel, he tried to think of anything but Sam. It was painful to know how easy it should have been to pick up the phone and bridge this huge gap he'd put between them. But he didn't have any words that didn't come out angry.

For three thousand miles, he thought about the time bomb that was his family and how Bill had sped things along. His anger was a huge, ever-growing pain that filled every part of his body. He tried to remember feeling as happy as he had last summer, and the loss of that feeling just made him angrier. He had to protect Sam from the ugliness inside of him. So he didn't call.

He had two thousand dollars saved up from summer jobs that would buy him a little time to find work. His plan was to bartend at a music venue while he found a way to break into the business. He had a catalog of exactly three finished songs that he wanted to record.

Looking back, it was madness. It was the specific kind of dreaming that belongs to a person who doesn't know any better. Like a ten-year-old who's sure he'll play in the NBA someday. All he had was a duffel bag and Dr. Nick's guitar, on his way to becoming a rock star. Even if someone had reasoned with him, he wouldn't have changed course. He knew that his future was in music the way he knew the sun was coming up tomorrow. But then again, he had thought his future was Sam too.

He found an apartment on Market Street in Venice Beach on Craigslist for four hundred dollars per month. It turned out it was just a studio apartment, one large room with his roommate's bed and a kitchenette in the corner. What passed for his bedroom was the walk-in closet, which had its own window and enough space for a twin mattress.

The building was on an alley that led to the busiest drug-trafficking street in Los Angeles. On either end of this alley were spectacular ficus trees with intricate trunks and root systems that tore up the sidewalks. Wyatt came to see Los Angeles in this light: beautiful and invasive, natural and violent.

His dream of bartending his way to success was an instant failure. There were no jobs in music venues for bartenders. There were no jobs anywhere for bartenders. He eventually took a job at a Shell station two blocks from his apartment and made minimum wage pumping gas, and more for minor car repairs. As he walked to work each day, he felt the flow of his life: playing guitar and fixing cars. Nearly all he'd ever wanted. Except Sam.

He liked to drive up to Malibu to surf at Point Dume and hear the music roll off the beach. The warm air, the gulls, and the cold water brought him back to Long Island. He thought about Sam and how he'd destroyed that last good thing in his life. It was as if everyone around him had let him down, so he figured he'd just finish the job. Wyatt stayed out on the water as long as he could, because there he couldn't help but be honest with himself. And when he was honest with himself, the songs came.

37

Sam

As her junior year wrapped up and the summer loomed, Sam dreaded going out to the beach. She'd never been there without Wyatt, and the thought of looking down the beach and not seeing him walking toward her with his surfboard, not hearing his guitar from the treehouse—it was enough to take her down for good. She daydreamed about picking up her phone and seeing a text: Meet me at the beach. And that daydream made her whole body ache. Her parents agreed to let her stay in the city for the summer, and her mother came back every few weeks to check on her. Sam worked as a hostess in a Mexican restaurant and saw herself and Wyatt in every couple that walked in and shared nachos. She tried to divine from their body language what it was that they were doing right.

WHEN SAM STARTED her senior year there was no doubt that she needed help, and she agreed to see a therapist. Dr. Judy let her talk for the first three sessions without saying much at all. Sam told her the whole story of their relationship and their families and the blowup. She confessed that she sometimes spent the hours between three and five a.m. staring at her phone, willing something to happen.

"Sometimes when my body is exhausted in the pool, I force myself to swim one more lap so he'll call. Or I tell myself that if I get to Fourteenth Street and the light is green it means he's going to call. I hold my breath a lot." Sam laughed a tiny laugh and pulled a throw pillow onto her lap. The piping was coming unraveled and she wanted to pull it right off. "I've gone crazy, haven't I?"

"A little bit," said Dr. Judy, leaning forward in her chair for the first time. "It's not your fault. You're addicted."

"To Wyatt?"

"Yes. To him and mainly the idea of him. You are addicted to the dopamine reaction you feel when you get a hit of him. This is typical of a user who became hooked on a substance during a critical time of development, and now that addiction is woven into your nervous system. You're well into your detox, and I am recommending no contact, which should be easy." Dr. Judy laughed at that last comment, which stung.

"You're putting me in a twelve-step program for heartbreak?"

"Kind of. You have an open wound, let's let it scab and then heal."

Sam stared at her hands. There was a raw cuticle on her right index finger that gave her a delicious spurt of pain when she worried it with her thumb. "But I love him. That's the whole point. You can't just make yourself stop loving someone."

"You're eighteen years old. You're not in love with this boy. It's youth and sex and excitement, all mixed up into an obsession. Technically, I'd call this an adjustment disorder. We have to get you adjusted to life without him and focused on something else."

Sam just stared at her.

"Trust me on this, and I can help you."

It seemed to Sam that she was probably right. She must have been addicted if the thought of never touching him again made her physically sick. Dr. Judy even went so far as to tell her parents to get her a new phone to break the visual and tactile association with Wyatt. Sam had to promise not to look him up. No Myspace, no Facebook. Sam liked the basic idea of this. She liked the idea that she had a disease that could be cured. She liked the implication that maybe Wyatt was bad for her. She felt a bit of relief in the way Dr. Judy minimized the whole thing, like she'd flicked the lights on in a horror movie to reveal that the bloody bits were just ketchup.

WHEN GRACIE WAS born in December, Sam dutifully visited her mother at the hospital. Bill placed Gracie in her arms without even asking. Sam handed her right back. Travis was home for the holidays, and the apartment was too small for a family of four plus a crying baby. Gracie slept in a bassinet in her parents' room, but the every-three-hours wailing seeped right into Sam and Travis's room and worked

Sam's already agitated nerves. It was her father who had caused the breakup, but in truth it was Gracie who was the last straw. Sam wasn't about to admit to Dr. Judy that she resented a baby, but there it was.

Sam babysat for the first time when Gracie was six weeks old. She woke up from her nap screaming, and Sam found her in her crib sweaty and red-eyed. "You stink," Sam said, lifting her up and placing her on her parents' bed to change her. Gracie looked Sam right in the eye, like she wanted to tell her something.

Sam grabbed the bottle her mother had left her and plopped onto the sofa with Gracie in her arms. She reached over to grab the TV remote and startled Gracie into a smile. Gracie looked up at Sam with the bottle between her gums and a big grin on her face, and Sam felt the hardness in her soften a bit. She leaned back and let herself feel the weight of Gracie in her arms, a whole human being with a whole future ahead of her. She wondered who was going to break Gracie's heart.

Sam started jumping in to help with Gracie whenever she could. She liked to wear the baby carrier on her chest while she walked around the city. She wore her dad's parka because it was big enough to close around the two of them, and she warmed her lips on the rim of Gracie's tiny pink hat. The weight of her and the smell of her made Sam feel like she was connected to something permanent.

When Gracie was three months old, Sam offered to take the bassinet into her room for a few nights. "You look exhausted, Mom. And I'm up anyway."

Laurel placed her hands on Sam's cheeks. "I'm so worried

about you. You need to start sleeping. You're going to fall apart."

"Ha. Too late. Just let me have her for a few nights. Leave me the three a.m. bottle."

The first night they shared a room, Gracie woke up at two. Sam had been lying awake listening to her breathe. There was a rhythm to Gracie's breathing that went well with the hum of the First Avenue traffic. Another thing she would have liked to have told Wyatt. Sam changed Gracie's diaper and settled back into her bed to give her a bottle. Gracie gave Sam a sleepy smile in thanks. Apparently, they both fell asleep, because the next thing Sam knew, it was seven and time to get up for school. It was the best night's sleep Sam had had in months.

Gracie became a permanent resident of Sam's room and they were both sleeping eight hours at a stretch. Sam and Dr. Judy started talking about things that were not necessarily Wyatt related—her college plans, her career plans, her mixed feelings about not going to the prom.

On a regular Tuesday session, Sam walked in with a large envelope. "I got into USC." The first thing she'd thought when she opened the mailbox was that she couldn't wait to tell Wyatt. She winced at the fresh pain.

"Oh," said Dr. Judy. "What does that bring up for you?"

Sam tried not to roll her eyes, but it wasn't easy. She assumed Dr. Judy endured a lot of eye rolling with comments like that. "On one hand it makes me excited. Like I could go to where he is and maybe run into him. Or he'd hear I was there and want to start over?" Sam ran her hand over the envelope like it was a pet.

"On the other hand?"

Sam looked over Dr. Judy's shoulder at the framed beach scene that was supposed to relax her but never did. "On the other hand, I know that's a fantasy and that if he wanted to see me he would have called me by now."

"Exactly."

Sam really did hate Dr. Judy just a little bit. "And when I think about it, going out there and not being with Wyatt would be a lot more painful than staying here. And being with Gracie."

Sam decided to give it up to the universe. If she got into NYU, she'd stay. If she didn't, she'd go to Los Angeles. As the end of March approached and the NYU decision was getting nearer, she started to realize that she'd gone from longing to see Wyatt to being terrified to see him. She was finally sleeping and spring was coming.

38

Wyatt

After ten months in Los Angeles, Wyatt's anger became more manageable. He knew he'd been harsh with Sam, and he knew he needed to apologize. He woke up in the mornings and imagined what it would feel like to have her there with him. He'd just written his first good song, and he wanted to play it for her. It should have been easy to reach out to her and tell her he loved her, but when he tried it out in his head, the way he felt about her still got all mixed up with how he felt about what happened. He didn't want to hear about how well her family was doing. He didn't want to tell her that he was still just surfing and pumping gas.

It was at this time that Wyatt saw a flyer at a music store for an open mic night at a bar in the Valley. He'd seen lots of ads like this before, but they were in Hollywood, in big venues that seemed impossibly daunting. The Valley felt anonymous, with a low risk of failure. Who cared if they didn't like him in the Valley? What did they know? It occurred to Wyatt, as he drove over the hill, that he'd been afraid this whole time. Working on cars while he waited to be a rock star was one thing, but actually trying and getting rejected was another. He wasn't sure he was prepared to find out that he was just a guy who works on cars. He knew that if Sam were here she would have forced him to try months ago. Sam was brave like that and unafraid to jump into anything. Of course, he didn't have Sam with him, but she was in his songs, and he hoped that would give him the courage he needed.

He arrived at El Roca at eight p.m., guitar in hand and sweating through his T-shirt. There were only about ten people seated at the tables in front of a small stage, half of them with guitars waiting to play.

"It's like this on Mondays," said the bartender. "That's why we do the open mic, to get musicians in here, hopefully thirsty."

"So much for my big break," he said. "I'll have a beer." He sat at the bar and listened to the other musicians and wondered what he was doing in LA.

He was working on his second beer and had mostly forgotten his guitar when the bartender said, "Holy shit." Wyatt looked up to see Carlyle Trickett, in dark glasses, find himself a table. At six foot five he was impossible not to notice, and with his perfectly cut silver hair he was impossible not to recognize.

"What the hell is he doing here?" Wyatt asked.

"He sometimes comes on his way home. He lives on Mulholland, I think. It's time you man up and take your turn there, buddy. This isn't going to happen to you twice."

Wyatt drained the rest of his beer and walked over to the side of the stage, where a woman with a perfect country voice was finishing her song. The musicians and a few of her friends clapped. Carlyle stared at the stage, disinterested.

Wyatt took the stage and sat on the stool behind the mic and started to play the new song he'd written on the water. It was about Sam and the way he felt like he'd taken her into his being. At the sound of the first few notes, he relaxed. He avoided the audience as he sang, singing for himself and seeing the notes as they came from his guitar. He could feel Sam everywhere around him, as if the song had taken him back to the happiest time of his life. *You catch your breath, and I catch your breath. We're locked in together. Sam, I am.*

As he played the last note, he felt certain that that song was going to change his life. He looked up at the applaud-ing audience and risked a glance at Carlyle, who was wav-ing him over. *This is it.* This was the moment where he was seen for what he was supposed to be, and the rest would be history.

Wyatt made his way over to Carlyle. "I'm Wyatt Pope," he said, extending his hand. He waited to be invited to sit.

Carlyle removed his glasses and did not invite him to sit. "The music sounds good, but you're not going to make it." It was now clear that Carlyle had been served someplace else before he made his way here. "The music is good—hell, the song is great—but your voice. It's just not enough to carry a band, not enough for a solo career. It's just not strong enough."

"My voice?" Wyatt was a little stunned.

"Yeah, I feel bad for a guy like you. Probably came out to LA to make it. I've been doing this for thirty years, I know a voice that will record. Yours isn't it. I thought you should know."

Wyatt had the odd sensation of being able to feel his heart. He stood there, nodding. "Well, if anyone would know, it's you. Thanks for telling me."

39

Sam

Sam was accepted at NYU on a day when she was the one to collect the mail from the lobby. She ran up the two flights of stairs to find no one was home. She opened the envelope and laid all of the pages out on the kitchen counter. WEL-COME TO NYU! She felt something like relief with a chaser of excitement; something was bubbling up in her and it felt like it might be the future. *Welcome to NYU!*

She couldn't wait to tell her parents. They'd be happy she was staying local and thrilled to take advantage of the tuition break that her dad got as a professor. She should call them. Her phone rang in her backpack, as if to answer her question.

It was Wyatt.

God's messing with me. That was the first thought she had when she saw Wyatt's name next to a years-old heart emoji pop up on her phone. She hadn't gotten the green at Fourteenth Street on her way home. She hadn't done an extra lap in the pool. Of course he would call the exact second she felt like it was possible to move on. It rang three times before she accepted the call.

"Wyatt?"

"Hey."

She was silent for a second, just letting the sound of his voice land and fill her head.

"Sam?"

"I'm here. Have you been stuck in traffic or something?"

Wyatt let out a little laugh, but it wasn't the happy laugh she remembered. There was pain to it. "Yeah, it's been a long time."

"It's been twelve months, if you haven't been keeping track."

"Yeah. I'm sorry about that."

This sounded to Sam like something you'd say when you bumped someone's shoulder in the hall. Not after you'd totally abandoned a person who was in love with you.

"How's LA?"

"Fine," he said. "I mean, not fine. I guess that's why I'm calling."

Sam felt her heart open up, right back to that place where she would do anything for him, where she loved him so much that the thought of his not being fine actually hurt. "Why? What happened?"

Wyatt let out a breath. "I tried. I guess that's what happened. I've just been surfing and writing songs and pumping gas since I got here, kind of imagining myself as a rock star."

This was exactly what Sam had been imagining him doing, though also waiting tables. She was lying on the couch now with her eyes closed, taking in the sound of his voice. "So what did you try?"

"Last night I went to an open mic thing in the Valley. There were a bunch of shitty bands performing, and I got up and sang a song I wrote."

"That's good, right?"

"Well just my luck, this big record producer was there, and he went out of his way to tell me that my voice sucks."

"He did not say that, there's no way."

"Okay, well, he said my voice could never carry a band and wasn't strong enough to record well, which is a nice way of saying I suck."

"I'm sorry," she said. Sam loved Wyatt's singing voice, but she knew enough not to say so because it would sound like something your mom said to try to make you feel better.

"Yeah. So I guess now I'm a guy who surfs and works at a gas station. Not an aspiring rock star. I feel like I have nothing left."

"I know the feeling," Sam said, looking up at a crack that ran halfway down the living room ceiling. It reminded her of the crack in her bedroom ceiling that she'd spent the past year staring at, willing it to spontaneously close and heal her. Dr. Judy was trying to get her to stop all this magical thinking. She sat straight up on the couch. "Wait. Why are you calling me now?"

"I guess I just woke up sad," he said. "I needed someone to talk to."

Sam heard the strangest sound come from deep in her throat. It was a laugh, but a hard laugh; if a goose could laugh, it would have sounded like this. "You needed some-one to talk to? You?"

"Yeah." Wyatt sounded small and clueless. And selfish. Sam could feel her heart constricting. She did not want to comfort him.

"I don't know how to break it to you, Wyatt, but I've also needed someone to talk to. You see, my boyfriend, who said he loved me, who was my whole fucking life, just kind of dropped off the face of the earth. Not really sure who I was supposed to call to get through that. It's not like you were picking up the phone when I needed you."

"I know, Sam. It was a hard time for me too. I'm sorry."

"You're sorry." Sam remembered how ineffective these words were when her dad was apologizing to her mom. She felt the sloppiness of these words, a casual nod to the rubble after you've totally destroyed something. Sam paced the length of the living room and felt the anger spread throughout her body.

"I am. And I want you to forgive me because I really need you right now."

Fireworks. Cataclysmic explosions. Sam could feel all of this anger erupting. She felt it burning through any last bits of depression or longing, and she was startled to discover that she was smiling.

"I needed you then. So you don't get to come back for me now." She heard the front door open, and her parents rolled Gracie's stroller into the living room. "And in other news," she said, smiling at her parents, "I got into NYU today. So that's what I'm doing. Don't call me again." And she hung up.

"Darling! That's fantastic!" Laurel said, taking her in her arms.

Bill dropped his backpack and joined in the hug. "I'm so proud of you, Sam." When Laurel was in the kitchen inspecting the proof of her admission, Bill asked, "So who was that on the phone?"

"Nobody. Absolutely nobody," said Sam.

PART 2

NOW

40

My mother serves margaritas before dinner, and I only have half of one. They are that deadly kind of margarita that tastes so sweet that it leaves you wanting tortilla chips and another margarita. I've learned this lesson, so I switch to water. Jack, as it turns out, has not learned this lesson.

Jack has a strict two-drink maximum, but he has three margaritas that I see, maybe more. "These are delicious," he says at first. "These are delicith," he says later. Jack rests his hand on my shoulder as Gramps grills my dad about his art sales.

"So how's the art world? You still making those big swirly things?" Gramps has never understood my dad's work and can double over laughing when he talks about how people were conned into paying good money for it. This has never bothered my dad a bit.

"Not lately," he says. "People want straight lines and earth tones, they tell me. It's taking me some time to connect to that." He looks out at the view his swirly paintings paid for. I feel myself soften as I watch him. For a long time

I felt like his dry spell was an appropriate punishment. But looking at the earnest way he searches the horizon for an idea, I miss seeing him thrive. "Takes time," he says.

"Must be nice," Jack says.

"It is nice," Hugh says, measured. "Doing something you love. You must feel that way about being a doctor."

"I guess. But digging skin cancer out of goddamn sun worshippers all day, I wouldn't do it for free."

This feels overly negative for a sunset barbecue. I say, "Well, I like my job."

"Bossing people around?" Travis says. "It's like they invented a whole industry for you." I laugh, remembering all of the summers I orchestrated adventures on the beach. A race to the jetty, the sandcastle contest. A million games of Capture the Flag. Of course, back then I just made up games because I wanted to play them. Now I organize people to keep them in line.

"Ah yes, Sam and her flash mob." Jack gives me a sleepy smile, and I hope to God he's not going to say any more about this. "I'm going in," he says, and kisses the side of my head.

I should go with him and make sure he gets to bed okay. But the weather is perfect and Granny's made pesto.

BY ELEVEN O'CLOCK Travis and Hugh have gone home, and everyone is in bed. I try to read *Wetlands of Westerleigh* and find myself reading the same sex scene six times. I can't understand where the body parts are in relationship to each other. He has both hands on the back of her neck and is pulling her hips toward him. How many hands does this guy have? I realize I am missing the point and should go with the feel of the whole thing. I wonder whether if I read this to Jack he'd think it was funny or if he'd just say, "Someone should have caught that."

When I think of Jack with his perfectly shaved face and aqua blue eyes, I wonder at the improbability of the two of us ending up together. Sometimes I follow this train of thought in the middle of the night, watching him sleep the sleep of a man who's worked a full day and exercised twice. For sure we are together because of Jess Landry, a secretary at Human Corps. The office threw her a baby shower on a Monday in the conference room. They'd over-catered and I was mildly broke, so I wrapped up two extra sandwiches and left them in the shared refrigerator for my Tuesday and Wednesday lunches, which is why I showed up at my Thursday haircut with thirty extra dollars for the extravagant blowout. Which (I'm positive) is the only reason Jack ever for one second considered me to be a person he might date when I got into that cab.

The million times I've traced back what brought Wyatt and me together, I get as far as my dad's painting *Current* and making all that money so he could buy this house. If *Current* was actually inspired by that old sky-blue VW Bug, then I guess it was the moment he bought that car. Something as tiny as a Bug or Jess Landry's fertilized egg could change the course of a person's life. Or something as huge as a shift in the weather pattern that heats up the East Coast enough to make a boy fill the water bottles at the house with the ice-cold water. I am overwhelmed thinking of all the factors beyond my control that have conspired to change the course of my life. I really hope they'll let me keep my job.

Wyatt's in the treehouse. He's just started with a slow melody, and it reminds me of the ocean. I'm putting on sweatpants and a sweatshirt over my nightshirt and am walking out the back door before I've really thought it through. My mom is right: we need to get it all out in the open and then bury it safely. And with Jack on a once-in-a-lifetime bender, this may be my only chance. I make my way into the Popes' yard and see his feet dangling over the side of the treehouse. I am up three rungs of the rope ladder when he stops playing.

"Sam?" he says, before I'm all the way up.

"Hi," I say. "I heard you playing and I couldn't sleep. I just wanted to . . ." My eyes focus in the dark and I take in the treehouse. The splintery floor has been swept clean. There's a blue and green striped rug in the center and a futon folded up in the couch position on the left-hand wall. Next to it is a small table, like a TV tray, with a lit candle on it. To the right, there are three acoustic guitars mounted on the wall, next to a well-used broom. "I don't understand."

"Come on in," Wyatt says, standing up, and we both start to laugh.

"Seriously, do you live here?"

"I do not. I mostly stay in the house."

"Then why all this?"

"I don't know. It's my favorite place. I fixed it up a little. I didn't want to leave it behind." These words land heavy on my chest. He left me behind.

I sit down on the futon. It's simple, and I can see how

this can all be dismantled when he goes, but this space has been put together with a lot of care. I flash on Wyatt's wanting to frame my drawing, wanting to keep it nice.

"Can we talk for a sec?"

"Sure." He sits down next to me, but not close. You could fit a fully grown Labrador retriever between us.

"I know it was a long time ago, but I just wanted to say I'm really sorry we ended in such a bad way, at such a bad time."

Wyatt seems surprised. "Me too," he says.

"And I wish I'd been less hurt so I could have come back into your life. That had to be really hard with your family. And your career and everything."

"It was," he says. Then, "This is the best part of you. The part that just says what needs to be said."

I don't know why he's being so calm when I'm feeling so nervous. "Now I forget what I needed to say."

"You're sorry we're not friends?" Wyatt offers.

That's not it, really. "It was hard for me. Losing you," I say.

"Travis told Michael you were fine."

"Travis knew I wasn't fine." I look directly at him and wonder if he can see on my face the remains of just how not fine I was.

"I didn't know how to come back here," he says. "Or how to reach out to you after I was so harsh. And then you were so harsh." He looks down at his hands, presumably for a cheat sheet to get him through this moment. He finally looks up at me and says, "I remember exactly what it felt like when we were together, and it's unbelievable to me that

I could have shut you out like that. I was a mess, and I know it's not an excuse, really, but I was eighteen." He leans back on the couch like it's perfectly normal for us to be having this conversation. All these years later. In his swept-clean treehouse. "Are you over it now?"

I let out a little laugh. "What a question. I'm getting married." I stare at my hands, twisting my engagement ring. "I guess I'm ready to be over it. Everyone has moved on. You have a life with your music and fixing cars, a lounge singer."

Wyatt laughs, "She's not a lounge singer."

"Whatever. I want her to be. She smells like smoke and her evening gowns are tired."

"She sometimes smells like smoke, and we're not really a couple."

The humidity has made my hair unruly and I busy myself by braiding the chunk that has fallen in my face. I can feel Wyatt watching me.

"How are your parents?"

"They're fine. Both remarried."

"Michael?"

"Good. Sober."

"Good. And you like your life?" I ask.

"I get to do things I love every day. The weather's always nice."

"Wow, that's so Zen. Self-actualized."

"Not really. What about you? Is your life what you wanted?"

I turn to face him, crossing my legs on the sofa. The space between us has shrunk. "Well, I've sort of screwed up my job. But I love living in the city. I get to see Gracie all the time, which is awesome."

"Get a new job."

"I'm probably going to get fired. Don't tell my parents. They'd love it too much."

"They'd love that you were getting fired?"

"Well, I think my dad can't get used to the fact that I have such a 'tight-ass job.' His words. He'd love that I blew up my whole career by blurting out two words when my whole job is keeping employees in line."

Wyatt laughs. "What were they, 'tight-ass'?"

"'Flash mob,'" I say, and cover my face with my hands.

"Oh God."

"I was working with a client who was trying to get his team to work more cooperatively. There are exactly three right solutions to this problem in our company manual: send them to a ropes course, give them a series of puzzles to work through together, administer an enneagram test. I've recommended these things a hundred times, and I'm just sick of them."

"So?"

"So I was sitting in this meeting and everything felt like an itchy sweater. I was having a hard time concentrating, and I couldn't stick to the script. There had to be a more fun way to get people to work together. So I said 'flash mob.'"

"'Flash mob'? Seriously?" Wyatt's smile is so big, like this is the best thing he's ever heard.

"It just came out. 'Flash mob.' It was like a fart in an elevator, there was no taking it back and it sort of filled the space." This has never been funny until right now. Seeing Wyatt laugh and hearing the words come out of my mouth, I feel laughter move all the way through my body. My shoulders are shaking and I have to wipe my eyes and nose on my sweatshirt sleeve.

"So," says Wyatt when he's caught some air. "They did it?"

"Yep. My boss was horrified, but she couldn't disagree with the client, who loved the idea. And once I'd suggested it, it was my problem. I had to choreograph the whole thing, to 'Dancing Queen.' Which was also my suggestion, I have no idea why. And then they wanted gold pants. It was a total nightmare. I could have just sent them on a ropes course and watched."

Wyatt is leaning back on the sofa, looking at me like I'm sixteen. He looks amused and delighted, and I can't remember the last time I was amusing or delightful to anyone.

"Thirty people in the lobby dancing in gold pants. It's like with two words I unwrote the firm's entire mission statement. The client loved it, but of course my boss is out of her mind because I went so completely rogue and it cost us so much time." My head is in my hands, and I'm not laughing anymore.

"You really never thought any of your ideas through to the end."

"That hideous tree on my wall is a case in point." I look up at him. "So, the not-so-funny part is that things aren't looking good for me at work. There's a chance I'm going to lose my job."

"Seems worth it to me," he says.

Hardly. If I could go back in time and snatch those two words back, I would. But just talking to Wyatt about it makes me feel better, and I briefly wonder if Dr. Judy would tell me that this is what addiction looks like. A quick euphoria after having the thing you've been craving. I start to feel like maybe it was the friendship that I was mourning all those years. There is not one person on earth I can open up to like I can to Wyatt.

The laughing has brought us closer together on the futon. I mentally measure the space between his thigh and my knee.

"Tell me about your girlfriend."

"She's seriously not my girlfriend. It's more like a work arrangement."

"You don't even have a job." I don't like the way this sounds, so I study his face to see if it stung. It didn't. He seems completely at peace, with himself and with me. He puts his hand on his thigh, and I resist the urge to touch it. It's the same but not the same, and I wonder if the feel of it would still change my skin into something else. "But you have health insurance, right?"

Wyatt laughs a big laugh. "I do."

"Good," I say, and I can't stop myself. I reach over and take his hand in mine. It's not like I'm holding his hand but more like I'm examining it. I run my fingers over the back of it and then trace them over his palm. I know immediately that this was a horrible mistake, because I can feel my skin melting into his, exactly the way I remember it. I cannot take my hand away, but I am afraid. This thing, this childhood madness, left me so broken. It's taken me a decade to create a life that feels safe. Touching Wyatt makes me afraid I'm going to rip the seams out of everything I've sewn.

He stops me by placing his other hand over mine. "Maybe you should go, Sam-I-am."

"Yeah," I say. "Do you like that song?"

"I do," he says. "Now get out of here."

41

"You slept late," is all anyone is saying to me. I did. I slept until nine o'clock and through a surfing date with Gracie. Even Jack's up.

"How was your trip to Margaritaville?" I ask, giving him a hug.

"I don't know how that happened," he says. "I'm sorry. I feel like crap."

"Want me to make you a Bloody Mary?" asks Granny.

"No, thank you," he says.

"I'm so sorry," I say. "Mom's margaritas are deadly. I should have warned you. Want to jump in the ocean real quick? It might help."

"I need to get out of this sun." Jack makes his way back out the front door and up to the garage apartment.

Since Gracie and I missed the waves, we take our surfboards out to just float around. I feel a small tilt in the Earth's axis, a combination of mild anxiety and glee. I'd really like to talk to my mother. I need to tell someone that I made a quick trip back to myself and felt easy for a while.

But if I told her exactly how open Wyatt and I were and how much we laughed, I'm afraid she'd panic. To my mom, Jack is more than a fiancé, he is the bubble wrap that she'd like me to wear.

Gracie and I are floating around when she sits up on her board and waves her arms at the shore. Her eyes are better than mine, but I can tell from the motion we're getting in return that she's waving at Wyatt. In minutes he's paddling out to meet us.

"Hey," I say, and roll onto my back so I don't have to look at him.

"Jack's hungover," Gracie tells him.

"Good for him," says Wyatt.

"He doesn't really like being a doctor."

"That's too bad."

"He doesn't like the sun or the ocean."

"What does he like?"

"Margaritas, I think."

They laugh.

I am hypnotized by the feel of the salt water and the sound of its lapping against my board. The sun is prickly warm on my face, my chest, my legs. As I let my feet dangle in the water, I am aware of every inch of my body, every breeze that cools where the sun has gotten too hot. I try a thought out in my mind: *Wyatt and I are going to be friends.* He was the most important person in my life, and I have grieved over it forever. I took all of my pain and disillusionment from my dad's affair and wrapped it up in that one loss. Now he is resurrected in the form of a really nice guy who is also friends with my little sister. I just have to not want to touch him. It would be like drinking nonalcoholic beer, all of the taste without the buzz. *Take that, Dr. Judy.*

I listen as she tells him about volunteering at the animal shelter after school so she can get a job handling dogs at the vet's office. Those are the first few steps in her twenty-step plan to becoming a large-animal veterinarian. Wyatt's saying that sounds like a lot more work than making up songs.

I've heard all about both of their dream jobs, but there's something about hearing them tell each other. Gracie was the last straw for Wyatt; the fact of my mom's pregnancy pushed our fragile relationship over the edge. Wyatt is before, and Grace is what came after. And if they coexist on the same plane, maybe all there really is is the now. It's possible I've had too much sun.

"I want to be an art teacher," I say in my quietest voice. I say it almost to myself.

"What?" asks Gracie. "Did she say something?"

Wyatt says, "She said she wants to be an art teacher. Sam, that's such a no-brainer."

I feel too exposed lying on my back and turn over. "I'm not qualified at all, but I'd really like to work with kids and help them make stuff. I always think about that when I come out here and then forget about it when I'm back in the city."

"You'd be good at that," says Gracie.

"You should totally do this. Like now." Wyatt sits up, straddling his board.

"It's not that easy. I'd have to go back to school."

"You don't seem that busy," Wyatt says.

I hate myself for bringing this up. I have no idea what would have possessed me to tell them this. The sun, the water. I must have gone into some kind of fugue state. And then with a mercy only the ocean could provide, the waves start to pick up.

"SOMETHING'S HAPPENED TO you," my mother says.

"Lots of things have happened to me," I say. "I'm thirty."

"Okay, we don't have to talk about it."

We're unloading the dishwasher, wiping the plates and glasses dry because this particular forty-year-old dishwasher no longer provides that service. "I feel better," I say. "I talked to Wyatt."

She clutches the mug she's drying to her chest and leans back against the counter. "Tell me."

"I went to see him last night. In the treehouse." I say this last bit to the worn wooden floor. "And we talked."

"About what?"

"Not so much about what happened. I think we're just chalking that up to being young and not knowing how to deal. But about our lives now, I guess. Sort of the way we used to be able to talk for hours about nothing. I think I missed that."

"Oh. So that's nice?" She's re-drying the dry mug. It occurs to me that my mom may have more than a little bit of PTSD about my prior Wyatt meltdown. Her life was in a free fall, and I kindly piled on the way only a teenager can.

"It was. But it's nothing to worry about. We are going to be friends, I think. And I think I forgave him. And he forgave me. I feel like I've put down something heavy I was carrying."

"And that's it? The whole story?"

"Mostly," I say.

42

It's Saturday and it's our last day on Long Island. For me, this means that tomorrow I'm going back to the city to figure out my life. It makes me a little panicky thinking of the possibility of the rest of the summer without a job, wandering around that hot city alone with absolutely no plan, while Jack keeps crushing his leg day, push day, and successful-doctor routine. I'm also unsettled about Wyatt. We've opened the door for some kind of a friendship, but it's maybe too new to work long-distance.

For my mother, it means that tonight is the last stop on her already successful mission to make Jack love Long Island. At noon she calls the Old Sloop Inn to tell them we'll be nine for dinner. They inform her that they've been booked for a month because the music festival is starting tonight.

She is entirely thrown off by this. It's not just that her dinner plans have been crushed, it's more like all of her plans have been crushed. I wonder now if this push for us to get married out here is about much more than the wedding.

Maybe, she thinks, if Jack likes it enough, then I'll start coming back more during the summer. Our wedding is the magic potion that will bring me back to Long Island for good.

I hear my mom on the phone with Travis: "This is a disaster. We have to eat there tonight so they can see it all lit up. Can Hugh do something?" I know this bugs Travis, Mom's suggestion that Hugh is more plugged in than he is. "Wyatt? What could he do?" she asks.

And that's how it came to be that my mom asked Wyatt to help us get a dinner reservation, not just for the nine of us but for ten. Wyatt had to assure them he was coming.

"What, did he fix the maître d's car or something?" asks Jack.

"It must have something to do with his helping get the music festival here. The whole town owes him," my dad says. The whole town does seem to owe Wyatt; it's a huge thing to have the festival here. I wonder how Wyatt ever came to know the people who are organizing it or why they listened to his suggestion for a venue. It seems like if he has those kinds of connections, someone would be able to help him break into the business.

"I don't know," my mom says, "but I am so relieved. You guys will really get to see what the place looks like full of people, all done up."

"You've mastered the hard sell, hon," my dad says.

"In case you missed it, I'm already sold," says Jack. He's in a Panama hat and long sleeves in the shade of the back porch. He hasn't once set foot in the ocean. I try to reconcile these facts—Jack loves it here and has not engaged at all with the beach. I wonder if it's possible to stay buttoned up at the beach—whether I could come back here freely for the rest of my life without regressing back into an impulsive kid.

IN CASE ANYONE forgets I'm the bride, I wear a long white linen dress. I've gotten a little sun this week and the color reminds me of someone I used to be. I look healthier, more vital. Jack just shakes his head when he sees me.

Travis and Hugh are waiting outside when we arrive. "It's packed in there," Travis says. "Granny's not going to be able to hear anything."

"Sometimes those are the best nights," Granny says.

We walk in and my dad greets the maître d'. "Hello, Maurice. You couldn't take nine of us, but now we are ten. Pope party."

"Of course, we have you tucked along the back wall there. Is Mr. Pope here?"

As we all stop to ponder who he could possibly be talking about—Frank is in Florida, after all—Wyatt walks in. Wyatt's in a pink button-down shirt made of the thinnest possible material. I imagine I can see through it and my mind goes quiet.

Wyatt greets Maurice warmly. A tall man with a full head of silver hair walks over and shakes his hand. We're all introduced; his name is Carlyle. Wyatt introduces me as Samantha rather than Sam, which is strange and oddly formal.

"Well, you were right," he's saying to Wyatt. "This is better than Newport. It feels fresh and we'll see the first bands tonight at that old barn, which is less horrible than I'd imagined."

"See? You've got to listen to me more often," says Wyatt.

"I would if you didn't have such a shitty singing voice," says Carlyle, and, inexplicably, they both start to laugh.

We make our way to a long table in the back and find our seats in a haphazard way, but when we're seated, I realize that we've fallen into our old habit of sitting with all of the kids at one end of the table. Wyatt is directly across from me. The first time I look up and catch his eye, he is giving me a look that says, *See? Isn't this easy? We made up, we're friends. Go ahead and get married.* I realize that's a lot to take from a look.

"So what do you two think?" Hugh is asking. "Cocktails outside in the garden? Dinner and dancing in here? Or cocktails upstairs in the bar?"

"I'd do the whole thing on the beach," says Wyatt.

Jack ignores him. "I love this place."

"What about you, Sam?" asks Travis.

I look around the room and am suddenly hot, like heat is coming from my chest up to my face. I want to say it's perfect. There's nothing to do but go back to the city and plan this wedding. I'll learn how to waltz, stepping exactly in time within the confines of a box, memorizing specific guidelines for how my body should react to music. I can feel the gentle pressure of Jack's hand on my back, telling me which way to go. One-two-three, one-two-three, on and on forever.

"I think I'd like a martini," I say.

43

"How do you know Carlyle Trickett?" Jack asks Wyatt over dessert.

"You know who that is?" I ask.

"Well, yes," says Jack. "He's the biggest record producer in LA, has been for decades. He just gave up forty-five million dollars in a divorce. You should really read the *Post*." *I would,* I want to say, *but I'm slogging through some dead earl's fictional memoir.*

Wyatt says, "I met him in a bar in the Valley when I was first in LA. He was pretty quick to tell me I had no future as a singer." He says this with a laugh, which makes no sense, and I check my martini to see if I'm drunk. No, it's still full. I don't know who I think I'm kidding, I can't drink a martini.

"I remember this," I say. "So mean."

"Maybe. But also maybe true. It's kind of nice when someone in show business tells you the truth. It's rare and can save you a lot of heartache."

"Yeah, I guess he'd know," says Jack. "Bummer."

This feels rude, but Wyatt is nonreactive. He shrugs in a *Well, what are you gonna do?* kind of way. He had this confidence as a kid, but it came from his abilities. He was a strong surfer, then a great guitar player. Maybe the best kisser ever. But I can't imagine that kid being okay with his dreams being shattered. Something feels false.

When we've finished eating, a couple stops by the table to say hello to Wyatt. They want to make sure he's coming by the Owl Barn later. He tells them he'll try to stop by. I know a few things: Jack's had too much to drink again and I've had three sips of a martini and a glass of white wine, which is getting close to too many for me. I'm in and out of conversations. My dad is thinking about a new series of paintings in straight lines that mimic the horizon. Granny wishes more people would say *You're welcome* rather than *No problem.* Travis and Hugh might get a dog. I'm leaning back in my chair, arms folded, mentally sorting through it all.

The waiter comes to the table to tell us that our meal was on the house, a small thank-you to Mr. Pope for bringing in all this business. My dad raises his glass to the waiter and then to Wyatt in thanks. And there's no surprise on Wyatt's face. I know every expression his face makes, and there's no hint of surprise there. I narrow my eyes at him from across the table. He looks away.

The fresh air feels good when we're out in the parking lot. My parents and grandparents get into my mom's car, and the rest of us are standing around Travis's. "I don't really want to go home yet," I say.

"Let's go hear the budding musicians!" says Jack with a bit of a flourish. He's definitely a little drunk.

"I'd do that," says Hugh.

We say goodbye to the old folks and Gracie and pile into the car. I'm in the middle of the backseat with Jack and Wyatt on either side. I am grateful when Jack puts his window down, because I need air.

Wyatt is looking out the window at nothing because it's completely dark. It feels like he's trying to put as much distance between us as possible in this tiny space. I turn to look at him and catch his eye. He just shakes his head and turns back to the window.

The Owl Barn is an actual barn. I've never been inside before but apparently it's been renovated as a music venue specifically for the festival. A band is playing country music when we walk in, and they're pretty good. The place feels crowded and smoky in the best possible way, like it's welcoming you in and making things a little hazy. A bartender comes out from behind the bar and gives us all beers. He gestures to the room and gives Wyatt a hug.

The band starts another song and Wyatt is listening intensely. He seems to notice my watching him. He turns to Travis and says, "I like this song," just like he would have years ago driving around in his dad's truck.

A guy in a Def Leppard T-shirt and a little red hat stands at the microphone. "That was 'Blackout.'" Everyone applauds again. "This just in—I see Wyatt Pope in the crowd." People start clapping and looking around the room. Wyatt raises his hand in the air, and the crowd erupts in cheers, which makes no sense. I look at him as he's taking this in and know that I'm missing something. "Let's see if we can get him up here. Just one song?"

He turns to me and almost says something before he makes his way through the crowd to the stage.

People are literally screaming as Wyatt gets on the stage. Red Hat brings him a guitar and a stool to sit on, and Wyatt examines the guitar like he's got all the time in the world. I don't see a hint of the nerves I would feel getting up there in front of all those people. "Everybody, Wyatt Pope." Applause, whistles, cheers, then silence.

Wyatt takes another second to adjust the guitar, then leans into the microphone. "This was my first break," he says. And then he starts to play. After three notes, the crowd erupts again, like it's a dream come true to hear Wyatt play Missy McGee's song. I know this song like I know my own heartbeat. *You catch your breath, and I catch your breath. We're locked in together. Sam, I am.* As he plays each line, the song sounds the way I always heard it in my head. It feels more country than pop. And it's no longer about Missy McGee's old boyfriend. It's about Wyatt and me. As he finishes and the crowd is screaming, he looks right at me, and I fully understand that I know absolutely nothing about him. And that he wrote that song.

My body is packed tight among the still-clapping fans, but my mind is everywhere. Wyatt told me he was writing songs in Los Angeles. I've even heard him writing songs in the treehouse. Why would he hide the fact that he wrote that song? I think of Missy McGee's other big hits and how similar they are to this one. Wyatt's been bullshitting me this whole time about his life. I'm both blown away by the song and angry at the lie.

Jack is at my elbow now. "Pretty good, right?"

"What?"

"Wyatt. That was something," he says. "He could get a gig somewhere. Not in the city, but like out here?"

I look back at the stage. Wyatt is looking directly at me, though I can't tell what he's trying to convey. Appropriate messages would include: *Hey, sorry I forgot to tell you anything about who I am* and *Hope you're not embarrassed about blabbing on and on about your dumb job when it turns out I'm a music industry icon.* And, *Yeah, I wrote the biggest song of the last decade and it was about you.* Really, the possible meanings are endless.

I need air. I'm in the center of the mob and am relieved to find Jack is still next to me. "I need to get out of here."

"Are you kidding?" he shouts. "This is unreal. I love this place." I must have missed the plaque that says SKIP WARREN SLEPT HERE.

I turn to fight my way out of the crowd and he doesn't notice. A rock band has replaced Wyatt, and they are warming up. Young people with plastic cups of beer let me pass without taking their eyes off the stage.

44

I hate this ridiculous white dress. I sit down on a barrel outside the barn, and I'm sure I'm getting rust stains or worse on the back of it. If I disappeared right now onto the beach, I'd be like the apparition of the dead bride in some Victorian novel. I think of all the times in my life I've been a cliché. Tomboy little sister. Lovesick teenager. Reluctant twelve-stepper. Right now I'm the runaway bride.

I google him. Wyatt Pope. He has a Wikipedia page. This makes my head spin. People should tell you right away. *How are you?* Answer: *I have a Wikipedia page.* It says a lot. I scroll through. The words "Billboard Top 20." So many times. On-again, off-again relationship with Missy McGee. For seven years. My Wyatt—and he is my freakin' Wyatt—has been dating the biggest pop star since Madonna.

I am a teenager. Not the teenager I was, carefree and reasonably happy in my skin. I am a teenager from TV, feeling embarrassed and like I'm trying too hard. I've been trying to sneak my old boyfriend back into my life, like I can carry him down the aisle with me, tucked under my bouquet with my tissue. That person, as it turns out, is too famous to sneak anywhere.

I text my dad: Can you pick me up? I'm at the Owl Barn.

My dad pulls up just as Wyatt walks out of the barn. He stands there in his pink shirt, looking at me and then the car, like he's trying to figure out his next move.

"You going home?" he asks.

I walk to the car and open the passenger door. Wyatt walks around to the driver's side, where my dad's leaning out his open window. "Need a ride, son?"

"Yes, thank you," he says, and gets in the backseat.

My dad asks, "So how was it? Music any good?"

"I hope so," says Wyatt.

"Yeah, it was good," I say. "And you know what else? Wyatt's a big star and he didn't tell us because maybe we couldn't handle it."

"Of course I didn't think that," says Wyatt.

My dad turns to me. "Big star?"

"Oh yeah, Wyatt who wanders around strumming his old guitar and tinkering with engines, he's a big secret success." I turn around to the backseat. "You were never going to tell me you wrote that song? And that you're dating fucking Missy McGee?"

He's quiet.

"I had to google you. Why didn't you tell me?"

"Ah, you googled me. Finally." He sits back and crosses his arms in satisfaction.

"Who googles people?" I ask.

"She was kind of in a twelve-step program," my dad says. "Googling would have been a no-no."

"Dad." He concentrates on the road. I look out the window.

"Really, Sam, how could you have ever heard that song and not known it was about you?" Wyatt asks.

I don't answer. Because I don't know how that's possible. Now that I know, I can't unknow it, like when you find the hidden tortoise in the *Highlights* magazine and then it jumps out at you every time.

Wyatt leans forward so that his head is right between us. "I figured you'd reach out to me when you heard it. Like maybe it would count as an apology."

"Ever try returning a text? It's more reliable than sending a secret message out over the radio."

My dad laughs, then turns to Wyatt. "Sorry." Eyes back on the road.

"What about 'Summer's End'?"

"About you. They're all about you, Sam."

"Well I'm glad to have provided you with material."

"What did you think I was going to grow up and write songs about? I've loved you my whole life."

"Okay, now I'm uncomfortable." My dad leans forward in his seat like that'll give us some privacy.

"I even asked you about that song. I was holding your hand. Were you looking for a better time to tell me?"

"I wasn't going to lay all that on you when you're about to get married."

"Well you did tonight."

"I did, and I don't know why." He leans back into the backseat, and my dad lets out a breath. "Listen, I know it sounds creepy, like I'm obsessed or something, but it's just that you were my big love. I write love songs, so I go back to that. But we're all grown up and you've found someone else. It's just a beautiful moment, like something you'd draw. I write songs about it."

"I don't draw anymore. 'Moonshine'?"

"About you."

"Wow."

Out of the corner of my eye, I can see my dad smiling. I'm not going to turn my head to confirm because that's going to annoy me.

We pull into our driveway, and my dad shuts off the car. "Okay, well I'm going in," he says, and quickly gets out. It's quiet and dark in the car; no one's put the porch light on. Neither of us makes any move to leave. I have nothing to say, but I'm not done. My heart falls when I hear him open the car door to leave. It's three seconds of regret before he opens the driver's door and sits next to me.

"Sam, look at me."

I turn to him and feel like there's the right amount of space between us. The gearshift and the cupholders are a barrier. Also the dark.

"It was really bad for me," I say. "I was in therapy for a long time. I didn't sleep for a year. And I lost a part of myself, the part that was true." I can feel tears on my cheeks.

"You're still you, Sam." He's looking me in the eye, and I believe that he sees what used to be there.

"I can't believe you wrote that fucking song," I say, and he laughs.

"I can't believe you didn't know."

"I just figured all young love feels the same. That at some point Missy McGee felt like we did." I shake my head at the sound of her name. "You probably don't call her Missy McGee."

He doesn't say anything.

"I'm happy for you," I say. "Your dream life and everything."

Wyatt lets out a little laugh, the kind of laugh that comes out to keep the next thing you say from seeming sad. "Wrong girl, and I don't get to perform. But the rest is pretty good." He takes my hand in both of his, and I can barely see them in the dark. "I know I hurt you, and I'm sorry. I'm ashamed of how broken I was. But we've both moved on. You're getting married and I want you to be happy."

It's the right thing to say. He's gently closed the door to the past, and we are now sitting here in the dark present. Yes, I'm getting married. I was still on Wyatt's mind all those years, but as an idea of what love was, something to write about. Like a particularly delicious donut on a cold morning. You remember fondly just how it tasted on your tongue, but today you'll order an omelet because you're a grown-up.

He lifts a hand to wipe a tear off my cheek. I feel myself leaning in toward the smell of him and the feel of his breath right there, inches from me. "It's ridiculous how much you want to kiss me," he says.

And I laugh because, yes. There's no point in denying it; Wyatt knows how to read every part of my body.

He smiles a tiny smile and takes both of my hands in his. "You mean the world to me, Sam, and I'm not going to do that to your life."

I look into his eyes and feel the warmth of his hands in mine. I know this will be the last time, so I take it in. "If I'd googled you and called, what would have happened?"

"It doesn't matter now, Sam."

45

We have Sunday brunch on the back porch, and I notice there's no music coming from the treehouse. Jack is saying how much he liked the Old Sloop Inn, how the crab cakes were the best he ever had. "Sam, I Am" is about me. All those songs are about me. I can't quite wrap my head around the fact of it and the fact that I didn't know. I wonder if he thinks of me every time Missy performs it, or if it's like "The Star-Spangled Banner" to him now, a bunch of words you've heard too many times.

"So it's a go then?" Granny asks. "Sam?"

I come to. "So what's a go?"

"The wedding?"

"Well, of course," I say, taking Jack's hand. "We're definitely getting married."

"Yes," my mother says, "we assumed that, dear. She means out here. Is it a go to have the wedding on Long Island?"

"For sure," Jack says for me. And I don't want to argue. It's beautiful out here, even if it's full of ghosts.

"Yes, I'll call and set a date as soon as we're back home," I say. Then, "Did you guys know Wyatt was a big deal in the music business? Like he's a success?"

"Like he has a band?" Granny asks.

"No, more like he's written a bunch of really big songs for a pop star, who at some point was his girlfriend," I say, scooping eggs onto my fork to avoid looking at anyone.

Jack says, "I have to admit I never saw that coming. He doesn't give off a vibe that would make you think he's got anything going on."

"It's news to us," my mom says. "Good for him."

My dad is watching me. He is the only witness to the conversation that Wyatt and I had last night, and I have the feeling that he didn't mention it to my mom. He's seen behind the curtain, and I like that he's protecting my privacy this way. I can't remember the last time my dad and I shared a secret.

"Yes, good for Wyatt," he says.

JACK AND I are quiet as we drive home on the Long Island Expressway. He's getting in and out of the express lane like he's trying to shave fifteen seconds off his best time in a race. I have an email from Eleanor saying that she'd like to see me in her office on Monday morning at ten. All this mystery is really getting on my nerves. After I was pulled off that client, I spent an entire week just sitting at my desk waiting for someone to make a decision about me. I organized my files. I color-coded a spreadsheet I'll probably never use again. And somehow they needed another week to mull it over without me there. It feels like Eleanor wants to punish me before she fires me. I reply, "See you then!" and immediately regret the cheery exclamation point.

I sneak looks at Jack and wonder what he's thinking about, staring ahead at the road. Is he as gobsmacked as I am about Wyatt? Did he like being out at the beach with my family? Did he get that that song is about me? He's millions of miles away, so I ask the annoying question.

"What are you thinking about?"

He turns to look at me, like he's surprised I'm there. "Elliot."

"Elliot?"

"Yeah, he needs to move our Tuesday evening tennis to Wednesdays. But Wednesday is my push day at the gym and if I switch it to Tuesday, it's too close to the Fritz workout for proper recovery."

"Ah," I say. "Tricky."

He keeps driving and chewing on his dilemma.

"Eleanor emailed. Wants to meet with me tomorrow morning."

"Good," he says. "Then you should take a few weeks off before you start looking for another job."

"I'm not necessarily getting fired."

He gives me a sympathetic smile. "Samantha. Come on."

I want to teach art, is on the tip of my tongue. Jack and I are getting married, I should be able to tell him my dreams. I just don't want to hear him tell me I can't, that it's impossible. That I've established myself as a consultant and I need to stick it out. It's not like I want to be a trapeze artist, I just want to be doing something creative with kids.

"I want to teach art," I say to the passenger window.

"Did you say something?"

"No," I say. Then, "I want to teach art."

"That would be fun," he says.

I turn to him, relieved. "Right? All those kids making things out of clay and construction paper. Everyone going in totally different directions with the same assignment."

"You could use a glue gun every day of your life."

I laugh. "Exactly. That's exactly what I want to do."

Jack reaches for my hand, and as dumb as that confession is, I feel heard. And if Jack thinks it makes sense, maybe it's possible.

"But you're an HR consultant. It's your whole résumé. So you've just got to make the best of that."

I'm quiet for the next thirty minutes, and as we head through the tunnel, I start to feel afraid. I've reconnected with Wyatt and we've said goodbye. I feel a dread that reminds me of the drive back to the city after Wyatt and I said goodbye on the beach, my mother seething. I have an irrational premonition that I will be abandoned and stop sleeping again. And Gracie's not coming back for a month.

I text Travis: I know you knew about Wyatt. It's unbelievable that you didn't tell me. We can fight about this later, but give me his number.

Travis: I figured if it mattered to you you'd google him

Me: Who fucking googles people

Travis: Everyone Sam

He sends it, and I text Wyatt: It's Sam. Travis gave me your number. Just wanted to say goodbye again. And wow. Also congratulations.

Wyatt: Ha, thanks. I'm headed back to LA tomorrow

Me: So can we be in touch? Like say happy birthday and send funny internet stuff?

Wyatt: Like cat videos?

I'm smiling at my phone and I check to make sure Jack isn't looking at me. He's not.

Me: Yeah, like that

46

I wake up on Monday morning in our bed on Sixty-Third Street. It's six, and I don't need to be anywhere until ten, but I get up anyway to have coffee and gather my thoughts. I close the door to our room quietly so as not to wake Jack. His first patient is at nine, I think he said. But first, it's push day. Or leg day. I forget.

I walk through our living area into the kitchen, and it's all a little stark after having been at my parents' house. "Clean lines" is what Jack said on repeat as we were looking to furnish this place. It's pretty, but it's a little ungrounding. I think of how Granny compared it to a prison. All this gray and white and chrome makes me wish there was something red to rest my eye on. It doesn't help that we are on the fourteenth floor, which everyone knows is really the thirteenth floor. We are high up enough that the cars down below seem like toys. I sometimes feel like I'm floating, like I'm inside someone's thought bubble.

I make my coffee and sit at the counter with my phone. I email my dad and ask if I can see photos of sketches from his new horizon series. This is pushy and presumptuous, as it's possible he still hasn't put anything on paper, but I do it anyway. I can't remember the last time I asked my dad about his work, but I feel a little opening between us.

I check to see if I've missed a text from Wyatt, which is dumb. We just agreed to stay loosely in touch. No one sends daily cat videos.

Jack comes out of the bedroom dressed for the gym. "Man, it feels good to be home."

"You said that yesterday," I say.

"Well, it still does. Everything's so damp at the beach." He stops to kiss me on the forehead before mixing his pre-workout drink. He doesn't have coffee because that pre-workout drink has as much caffeine as six cups, a thought that makes me slightly nauseated.

"I'm trying to figure out what to wear to my meeting this morning. Do I go casual because it's summer or do I dress up to be appropriate for the gravity of the situation?"

"The decision's been made; you could go in your pajamas if you want."

He's right, of course. Eleanor isn't inviting me in to negotiate. Jack's grabbing his gym bag and heading to the door. "I guess I'll call you after?" I say.

"Yes, sorry." Remembering himself, Jack comes back to give me a hug. "It'll be fine. There's tons of HR in the city." He pulls away and gives me a smile. "You'll be back to whipping people into shape in no time."

He leaves, and the words "whipping people into shape" hang in the air. I've never really thought of my job that way. I like to think I'm setting the rules for a game they can win, using data to keep score. I smile, remembering the moment everyone in the flash mob finally got the steps right. They were so excited about it, and I admit it was a little infectious.

I'm humming "Dancing Queen" as I refill my coffee and get back in bed. I have half an hour before I need to get in the shower and put on whatever one wears to get fired. I scroll through my phone. Emails from companies who think I should buy more sweaters. Ninety-six people liked my Instagram post of the Old Sloop Inn lit up at night. "Possible wedding venue," I said. I took that photo right before we walked into the restaurant. Wyatt must have been parking his car then, knowing full well that our dinner was being made possible by his celebrity.

I'm having a hard time knowing what is real. I survived losing Wyatt by believing that he was an addiction, that I was just boy crazy. But he wrote all those songs, with so many details of our relationship. He remembers it as clearly as I do. I need to look away from the possibility that what we had was real, because it could undo me. All of that laughing and touching is exactly the kind of freedom you'd feel if you threw yourself off a cliff. I don't want to be broken again.

I put down my phone and pick it back up again.

I text him: Are you up?

Immediate reply: A little jet-lagged so yes. How's life in the big city?

He used to say this, I remember, when we were apart during the school year. I'd smile when he asked it because it made me feel cool, like he thought maybe my city life was glamorous. I'm staring at those words now, uncomfortable with the way my body is leaning off the edge of that cliff.

Wyatt: Sam?

Me: Sorry, was just drying my hair. Life in the big city is pretty glamorous for an unemployed consultant

Wyatt: Did they fire you?

Me: I meet the firing squad at 10

Wyatt: I hope it goes well, but don't beg for a job you don't want. That's not who you are

Me: Easy for you to say, you're rich

Wyatt: Aren't you the one marrying a doctor?

Me: Haha. Okay I need to get moving, I'll text you later.

I don't know why that conversation has made me feel better. "Don't beg for a job you don't want" is great advice, and I take it to heart. That isn't who I am. I put my phone down and take in my bedroom. This is the space that Jack and I share. He loves the gray Roman shades on the windows and the matching club chairs at the foot of the bed. We both gravitated to the muted gray color scheme in the Pottery Barn catalog because it felt calm and sophisticated. But today it makes me feel like I'm in a military cafeteria.

I arrive at Human Corps ten minutes early. I walk through the lobby like I have a million times, but this time as I say good morning to Alvin behind the security desk, I'm preemptively embarrassed about the fact that I'll probably be back down in thirty minutes carrying a telltale cardboard box. I'm in a casual dress and sandals, mainly because it's ninety-eight degrees in midtown Manhattan, but looking down at my feet now, I realize I've never shown my toes here before.

I make my way to Eleanor's office, nodding hello to cubicled people who likely know my fate already. I knock on her open door and she looks up and smiles. A smile is a good sign.

"Sam, come in." She's in a black wool suit, because maybe she doesn't know about its being August outside. I take a seat across from her desk, which puts me a full inch lower than she is. Everything at Human Corps is by design, and I'm sure this is no exception. She leans forward and clangs her gold bangles on the desk. "This has been really stressful for me."

"I'm sorry," I say, and I don't know why. Am I sorry about the flash mob or wasting company time or just having inflicted work stress on my boss?

"Well it's been hell trying to explain this to management, how my best organizational consultant brought about sheer chaos."

"Chaos" seems a bit extreme. The whole song is less than four minutes. "Their dance was actually very well choreographed." I don't know where these words came from but they are out, and I cannot grab them back.

"Is that a joke?" Eleanor is clenching her folded hands.

"No. I mean, it doesn't matter now, but I was impressed with how well they all worked together. Which was what the client asked for." This is not going well. She is perfectly still, staring at me. I need to go back to the general "I'm sorry," but I'm just not feeling it.

"Do you want this job or not?"

It's a great question, and all I know for sure is that I

don't want to look for another job and have to explain over and over about the flash mob. "I do," I say.

She's looking at the floor as if she's trying to formulate the right words. She's making this overly difficult, and I wonder if this is the first time she's ever made a decision like this without a chart.

"You're wearing sandals," she says finally. "I've never seen you in sandals before."

"Yes, I hope that's okay. It's ninety-eight degrees out, though it's actually freezing in here."

"It's fine." She shakes off whatever conclusion she was coming to about the state of my footwear and goes on. "Purcell and I have decided we want to give you another chance. I know, we are not about second chances for our clients' employees, but we're making an exception here because you have a history of being exceptionally diligent."

"Thank you." I feel a "but" coming.

"For your next few projects, you will not be client facing. You'll be here sorting through the reports and data that you're sent. The first one is an analysis of employee health care costs, so it's all in black and white."

I have a feeling of being let back in, like I was on the outside and the circle has opened back up to me. I think of the girls at the beach going to that party without me and how it was okay because I knew I belonged with Wyatt, sitting there on the cove looking at the water while he buried my feet to keep them from burning.

"Sam, why are you smiling? I feel like you're not taking this seriously. You can keep your job, but we are course correcting. You shouldn't be smiling." If your job is micro-managing other people's behavior, it's hard to stop.

I realize that I need to end this meeting. I have been away for one week and it's like I completely forgot the script. "Eleanor, I love this job and I am so grateful for the opportunity to work with you and to make a difference for our clients. Just tell me when this next project starts and I'll be all over it."

"That's my girl."

I WALK OUT into the thick August air wondering how I'm supposed to feel. I still have a job. I just need to keep my head down for a couple of projects, and then they'll let me out in the world again. With less engaging work, maybe I'll even start making it to waltzing lessons. I feel no relief at all. Spreadsheets and waltzing lessons give me that itchy-sweater feeling all over.

I reach for my phone to text Wyatt, and as I start to type I realize how wrong that is. I text Jack instead, even though I know he's with patients: They didn't fire me, they're just going to torture me with boring work for a bit.

An hour later, I'm reading an unsanctioned work of women's fiction in bed when he texts back: Oh wow, I'm shocked but happy! I'll see you later.

Jack comes home from work with a bouquet of lilies. "I'm so happy and relieved," he says, wrapping me in his arms. "I know this whole wedding thing has been stressful. It was killing me to think you were going to lose your job over it."

I hug him back but then let go. "Wait. Do you think the flash mob was about our wedding?"

"Well, sort of. Not directly, but you've been distracted. Like forgetting appointments, doodling in your little book. You're not quite buttoned up, and I sort of assumed it was about the wedding."

I have in my mind the image of someone in a very long dress with buttons that go all the way up to her neck. She looks regal and polished and she can't quite breathe. I look down at my sandals and wonder if it's okay to just undo the top button every once in a while, without your whole life falling apart.

"I'm still buttoned up," I say. "Sometimes my mind wanders, but that's just what minds do."

"Mine doesn't."

I laugh and hug him again. "That's my favorite thing about you," I say into his neck.

"I want to hear all about your job drama. Let me change real quick and I'll take you out for sushi."

Jack goes in to change, and my phone buzzes. It's Wyatt: So?

Me: They didn't fire me but I don't get to have any human contact until they think I've learned my lesson

Wyatt: Ouch

Me: It's fine. This is what you get for farting in the elevator

Wyatt sends a string of laughing emojis, and, just like that, we have a new inside joke.

47

My parents have put down a deposit on the Old Sloop Inn for October 28 and we've ordered invitations. It feels like a concrete decision and it feels like everything is back on track. At least the wedding. I've started my analysis of a department store chain's health care offerings, and it's nine hours a day of mining data. My cubicle doesn't get any natural light, so I've started going to Central Park at lunchtime to try to catch a breeze and some bird sounds. On the Monday that starts the third full week on this project, I sit on a bench just outside the Central Park Zoo with a soft pretzel and a Coke. I find myself unable to move. Children are walking out of the zoo with ice-cream cones dripping down their little hands. A boy in a chicken costume points up to a bird that's landing on a balcony on Fifth Avenue. A man dances to music that's in his head, and if I watch long enough it seems like the squirrels hear it too. I am overwhelmed by how intensely I want to be where people are having ideas.

My mom calls. "Sweetheart, am I interrupting you?"

"I'm in a meeting," I say, breaking off a piece of my pretzel for a pigeon couple.

"I hear birds."

"Well, yes. So what's going on?"

"We need to get this wedding nailed down," she says. "The invitations should be arriving soon, and we have to start picking things out. Donna's called me twice asking for the color scheme, and I'm not entirely sure what she means."

Apparently, we are cutting things pretty close for an October 28 wedding. My mom wants us to come this weekend for Labor Day and to meet with the florist and taste the cake.

"Weren't we just there?" Jack asks when we're walking down Madison Avenue after dinner.

"That was three weeks ago."

"I'm not sure I can do two hippie beach visits in one summer."

I stop walking. "I thought you were the one who wanted to get married out there."

"Oh I do. I love it. But not the whole thing with your parents and that house and the stuff everywhere. The paint fumes alone took a year off my life."

"Huh."

"I figured the next time we went out it would be for the wedding. We'd stay at the Old Sloop Inn and then head out on our honeymoon. It's closer to JFK from there anyway."

I'm speechless, and I'm not even sure why. I may have thought that Jack's wanting to get married out there was a buy-in to the whole summer-at-the-beach thing. I may have even thought it was a buy-in to the complete picture of who my family is.

Jack puts his arm around me as we walk. "Listen, you know I love your parents. But them, out there, letting their freak flags fly, that's a once-a-summer thing for me. Can we make decisions over FaceTime?"

"We could. But it's our wedding. We're only doing this once. I'd like to taste the cake, feel the napkins, you know?"

Jack laughs. "Well, if you really need to taste the cake. You'll miss the US Open."

I've never been able to convey to Jack how little I care about tennis. I've probably never even tried, but you'd think he would have noticed that I'm the only person in the stadium not leaning forward in her chair with rapt attention.

"That's fine. You can take Elliot."

"That's a great idea," he says. "See how good we are at getting married?"

I TAKE THE train out to Long Island on Thursday night to avoid the Labor Day rush. Jack has parking passes to the US Open, so he didn't want me taking his car. I like the feeling of boarding the train by myself with everything I need stashed in my backpack. There's a little kid sitting behind me singing Christmas carols, and I know Wyatt would have something funny to say about that. I think it's okay to think that because we're friends now.

I text him: I think it's good that we're friends

There's no response. The train starts moving and soon

we're out of the city, chugging along past neighborhoods containing families with dramas all their own. I know there is a way to make my life something lighter. My parents are free spirits, and they've built a life that supports everything they want to do and be. Travis seems to be doing the same. I wonder what it would be like to be an adult who followed her spirit around, who just up and quit her well-paying job to start over as an art teacher. What if I could spend my time showing kids how to make things, how to access that part of your brain that is uniquely you and then use it to create something that people can see? Creating art is about being vulnerable enough to invite people to spend time in your skin. I can't think of a better skill to teach.

It occurs to me that Jack is a person whose skin I can't quite wear. I try to imagine his satisfaction at working his muscles so hard. I try to imagine his caring for patients he kind of resents. I try to feel how he feels about me, and I settle on hopeful. He loves me, and he seems hopeful that I'll figure out a way to get focused again. My phone vibrates.

Wyatt: We're friends? This seems so sudden

Me: Haha. I know, we've only known each other 25 years

Wyatt: Okay, well as long as you're sure you're not in love with me anymore

Me: I'm good.

There's no reply. I don't really like what I've said. It feels short and wrong. But then again, I am on my way to pick out wedding cake for when I marry someone else. I decide to double down.

Me: I'm on the train headed to Long Island. Going to

spend the weekend with my parents picking out tablecloths and tasting wedding cake

Wyatt: Did you decide to get married outside?

Me: Jack doesn't like the idea. It could rain

Wyatt: Let's hope he picks a good cake

Me: He's not coming. He had stuff to do, so I'm going to decide

There's no reply, not that that was anything important to reply to. I am a little disappointed, having thought maybe I was going to spend this whole train ride shooting the breeze with Wyatt. I'd really like to laugh. It's five o'clock in the afternoon in LA; maybe he's working? Or surfing? After twenty minutes, I get a text:

Wyatt: Well, I'll see you there. Coming for the long weekend to check on a few things for my mom. I'm taking the red eye, get in tomorrow morning

Me: Wow, okay. Meet me at the beach

That was a loaded thing to say. As soon as I send it, I feel embarrassed. We are trying to have an adult friendship, and here I am dragging up the past. He doesn't reply. My heart is racing a little and I try to breathe my way through it. *My friend Wyatt is going to be there this weekend. What a nice coincidence.* My mind immediately goes to what it's going to feel like when I hug him hello, burrowing my face into his neck. Maybe he'll write a song about it. These thoughts terrify me as they move throughout my body. *What a nice coincidence.*

48

Travis picks me up at the train. "Did you know Wyatt's coming out for the weekend?" I ask, like I'm just making conversation.

Travis smiles at the steering wheel. "I did not know that."

"He gets in tomorrow morning."

"Ah," he says.

"What?" There's really no one in the world who can use silence to convey as much ironic disapproval as a sibling. All that unspoken history fills the space.

"Nothing. Just interesting that he's turning up here. And you've somehow managed to leave Jack behind."

"Oh come on. Jack didn't want to come. He hates it out here." I've exaggerated, of course, but somehow I feel like I need to defend myself. It's not like I planned a weekend with Wyatt.

"He does?" Travis has dropped his edge. "What's there to hate?"

"'Hate' is the wrong word. He just prefers Mom and

Dad in the city, where they're a little more standard. Out here, the wacky house and all the stuff is a little much for him."

"That's who they are, Sam. That's like the best, happiest part of them. Jack's going to have to embrace it. And as much as you act like a tight-ass, it's a big part of who you are too."

We're on West Main Street now. Flags left over from Fourth of July are getting a second chance for Labor Day. A couple stumbles out of the Old Sloop Inn. We turn onto Saltaire Lane and pass Wyatt's house; no lights are on. Everything feels different than it did a few weeks ago, like without Jack as a buffer it's an actual step back in time.

We let ourselves in through the front door, and I allow myself to feel, maybe all the way down to a cellular level, how good it feels to be home. Everyone's asleep, and I smell garlic roasted potatoes that were likely burned a few hours ago. On the table by the front door is the usual assortment of mason jars, now with one full of rubber bands in different colors. I smile to myself, wondering if they're for a tie-dye experiment or for securing braids. With this crew, it could really be anything.

My mom's moved the dining room table back into the dining room, but it's still covered with driftwood and large pieces of peeled-off bark. There's a basket with a collection of sticks perched on a wingback chair. Travis finds me standing there, staring.

"You new around here?" he asks.

I laugh. "It looked like so much crazy garbage last time I was here. Now it just looks so happy."

Travis finds an open bottle of red wine on the counter next to a bowl of nuts and we take it all out onto the porch.

"Hugh can't stand it either, if that makes you feel better," he says.

"The house?"

"The stuff. He wants to kidnap them and take every last random piece of garbage and throw it out. He thinks that if Dad lived in a minimalist house, he'd be painting again. He daydreams about it."

"Clean lines?" I ask.

"Oh my God, it's all he talks about." We laugh.

"I like how they know what makes them happy," I say.

We're quiet for a bit, listening to the waves break. I've never been able to decide if the waves sound different at night or if there's just less noise to compete with them.

Travis says, "I feel like I should apologize for not telling you about Wyatt, but I'm not really sorry. It was hard for me, the thing with Mom and Dad and then seeing you totally fall apart. It was such a nightmare, and I was away at school, totally useless to you. By the time that song came out and Wyatt's life had changed course, you were finally okay."

"So you thought I'd fall apart again if I knew."

"I was afraid. And I waited two extra years to come out, waiting for you to feel normal again. That was a really hard time for me, and I figured telling you would start all the drama again. Maybe selfish in retrospect."

"I'm sorry." I never really thought much about how my falling apart affected Travis. I always pictured him having a big time in college, having escaped at the exact right moment. But I do remember all the calls to Mom to check in, the texts to me about absolutely nothing. He was taking our family's temperature and biding his time.

"But it's okay seeing him now, right? Like, it's good that you know all that before you marry Jack and move on with your mostly functional life."

"Mostly functional." I raise my glass to that. "Do you think Missy McGee knows she's singing about Wyatt's old girlfriend all the time?"

"I'm guessing no."

I COME DOWNSTAIRS in the morning feeling like it's Christmas. I don't know what it is, the fact that I have a free day at the beach, or the fact that I'm going to see Wyatt. The fact that my childhood home feels like home again. I want to grab a frozen peanut butter and jelly sandwich and run through the dunes. My mom's at the kitchen table watercoloring and smiles when she sees me.

"Is Gracie up?" I ask.

"She's started sleeping until ten. You remember how that was."

I smile at the memory of being twelve, almost thirteen. I wanted to sleep late too, but not as much as I wanted to get up and see Wyatt. "Oh, I remember."

"Something's loosened up in you. Nice to see."

"Maybe it's the sea air." I pour myself a coffee.

She gives me a long look. "That, yes. And also maybe spending more time out here this summer. Making peace. Finally getting over Wyatt."

I take a sip. "I think we're going to be friends. It's fine between us. Did you know he's coming here this weekend? Like today?"

"I didn't. Is that okay for you? Seeing him again so soon."

"I think?"

She gives me a look.

"I mean yes, it will be good to see him again. And maybe we can have a friendship of some sort." I think of a waiter warning me that the plate is hot. He's told me flat-out that if I touch it I'll get burned. And I touch it every single time.

My mom keeps painting, making wide ribbons of color across a stack of cards.

"What are those?"

"These came in the box with your wedding invitations, just extra card stock. I can't believe you ordered invitations on watercolor paper, it's so romantic."

"My invitations are here?" I get up and she indicates the three boxes under the dining room table. I grab a box and open it at the table. "I can't believe it."

They're beautiful. White cards with silver lettering. "Mr. and Mrs. Billings Holloway request the pleasure." Jack and I picked these out at the stationer on Madison and Eighty-Sixth Street. I gravitated toward an invitation with an engraved beach motif at the bottom. "Babe, it's a wedding, not a picnic," he said. So, we went with these, clean lines all the way. And he was right, they are gorgeous, and the little bit of texture in the paper saves them from being plain. We had them shipped to my mom, because, of course, she knows calligraphy.

"We have more than we need. Can I just show you something?" My mom takes one, dips her brush in the pink paint, and gives it a swoosh across the middle, accenting our names. It's breathtaking. "What if we did this to each one? All different colors."

"It is so pretty." I hold it in my hand and it feels like a summer breeze has moved through my wedding. "But Jack would think it was messy."

"Oh, okay. Let's skip it then. Maybe I'll just keep this one for myself. They're also very pretty without any color." My mom has no ego about her ideas or her art. She creates for herself, for the delight she feels in seeing something in a certain way or hearing the rhythm of the right words strung together.

As the pink is drying across our names, I think, *This is how I want my wedding to feel.* I want there to be a breeze sweeping across it, for it to feel fresh and like it's going somewhere. I realize, as I am thinking this, that I am imagining my wedding on the beach. But even at the Old Sloop Inn, we can be indoors and outdoors. It doesn't have to feel so stuffy. I stare at that watercolor swoosh and suddenly it represents everything I want my wedding to be.

"Do one more. I'll see what Jack says."

49

Wyatt's taxi pulls into his driveway an hour later, and I'm in my front yard cutting hydrangeas for the kitchen. His driver pulls away, and we stand there looking at one another from one yard to the next. I'm in shorts and an NYU sweatshirt. My hair is tied into an off-center bun on the top of my head. Not exactly my best look, and I'm pleased with myself for forgetting to care.

"Well, get over here," I say, dropping my flowers and walking over to give him a hug. I bury my face in his neck, just the way I imagined. I take in the feel of him, so casually pressed against me.

He says, "You already smell like the beach."

My arms are around his neck, and his hands are on my waist as he says this. We notice at the same time and take an appropriate step apart.

"How was your flight?" It's the thing people ask.

"I was up all night."

"No bed on your plane?"

"I don't have a plane."

"I bet Missy has a plane."

"Carlyle has a plane, that's it."

"Ah," I say. I want him to tell me what comes next.

"What comes next?" he asks. "I mean, what are all the wedding details you need to deal with?"

I take in a quick breath. "Okay, yes. There are a bunch of things."

"How much work could a wedding be? Do you have a dress?"

"It's in the city," I say, and scrunch up my face.

"What's that face?" He laughs. "Is it yucky? Smelly?"

"It's fine, it's sort of big and stiff." I don't know why I'm telling him this. "It's so fun that you're here. Want to go to Chippy's?"

"Sure. But don't you have a million things to do?"

"Not really. I mean I do, but all the appointments are tomorrow. I think my mom just wanted me here early for fun. What do you have to do for your mom?"

"It can wait," he says. "Let's get something to eat and then go look for waves."

"You want to go surfing?" I ask. I feel a current of excitement move through me. A whole free day on the ocean with absolutely nothing I have to do. A whole free day with Wyatt.

"Grab your stuff," he says. "What else are we going to do all day?"

WHEN WE'RE SEATED at Chippy's Diner with pancakes and a shared order of bacon, a comfortable distance from our usual table, I ask, "So are you going to write songs for that movie?"

"Have you been googling me?" Wyatt looks up from his plate and locks eyes with me, like he's caught me. I have to look away.

"A little. It's kind of addictive. *Variety* says they want you to write the whole score."

Wyatt laughs. "You're finally googling me, when we're in touch and you can just ask."

"I feel like I have to go back to the beginning and rethink who you are. It's like if I found out you were in a cult. Or a vegan."

"I swear I'm not so different."

"So do you own a house?"

"Wow, this really got personal."

"Seriously."

"Yes, I have a house in Malibu."

"Swimming pool?"

"No. But I can see the ocean."

"Nice." I'm picturing Wyatt at his house, looking out over the ocean. I imagine standing next to him there, looking at a beach that faces the wrong way.

"Michael lives with me, and there's enough room so we don't drive each other too crazy. Did you know he's becoming a therapist?"

"No. That's great."

"And he has a girlfriend he met in school. So she's there a lot too, which is fine because I'm at Missy's a lot."

"Oh." I take a too-big forkful of pancakes.

"Not like that," he says.

"What do you mean 'not like that'? We're grown-ups, Wyatt." I hold his gaze because it's fun that he's embarrassed.

Wyatt laughs. "I think there's some teenage version of me that doesn't want you to know I've cheated on you."

"I hate to say it, but I've been cheating on you too."

"You. You're getting married! I should totally break up with you. Or at least stop writing sappy songs about you."

My insides go warm at the thought of Wyatt's writing songs about me when I was in so much pain. As if that fact is retroactively healing. "Why can't Missy write her own sappy songs?"

"She doesn't write. When I played at the open mic for Carlyle and he told me my voice wouldn't record well, I was crushed. But I'd played 'Sam, I Am' and a year later he contacted me to buy it for Missy. That's how we met and my whole career started."

"Are you going to marry her?"

"I'm not even dating her."

"Come on."

"We've spent a lot of time together obviously. And sometimes we've been together." He is visibly uncomfortable talking about his love life. "The basic problem is we don't agree about anything, especially the music. From the beginning she was making my songs more pop than I like and now she's trying to record one with synthesizers, which, I mean, come on." He runs his hands through his hair like he's trying to wipe an annoying thought from his brain. He takes a deep breath. "She's a brilliant artist and all that, just not the kind of person I'm looking for."

"What kind of person are you looking for?"

"I don't know, Sam, just someone I like hanging out with. I'm not that complicated." He studies his pancakes. "This is your cue to change the subject."

"Okay, what about the cars? You said you still fix cars. Are you like Jay Leno with a fleet of Ferraris?"

"I drive a Toyota."

"So that was a full-on lie."

"No, when I was first in LA I worked at a gas station in Venice, pumping gas and fixing cars. This old guy Manny owned the shop and I kept checking in on him after I didn't work there anymore."

"That's not fixing cars."

"A few years ago he was in financial trouble so I bought the place and hired him to run it. And I do go by sometimes to help."

I lean back in the booth, taking him in. Wyatt. The goodest of all the good people I've ever known.

"So where do you want to look for waves?" he asks.

50

We secure our surfboards to the top of Marion's station wagon and make our way along the coast. Wyatt drives to Garnet Bay, to the same spot where he told me he loved me for the first time. I wonder if he remembers this as clearly as I do.

At the shore, we take off our shorts and T-shirts and avoid looking at one another. We carry our boards into the ocean and paddle out to waves that are bigger than I expected. Most of the surfing that I've done in the past decade has been this summer, and currently my whole life is off-balance, so I'm relying on muscle memory and good luck.

Wyatt takes the first wave he likes, and I wait. He paddles back to me. "What are you waiting for? An invitation?" He splashes my board.

"The waves are kind of intimidating," I say.

"You've got this, Sam. Come on." He turns away from me and paddles out, like he's not going to entertain my nonsense. He thinks I'm still that girl who's great at Capture the Flag.

I take the next one that comes along and fall pretty quickly. But it feels good, and when I come up for air, I am smiling.

"See?" he says. And we paddle back out.

I fall a bunch of times, but I don't really care. I like the feel of the water on my skin. I like the feel of the sun warming me just enough that the water feels cold when I go under again. The soundtrack of the ocean is in my head, and it replaces my to-do list and my nagging fear of waltzing in a box. I can move however I want in the ocean. I'm completely free.

Wyatt paddles over to me. "You getting tired?"

"A little." We're on our stomachs, and he's holding on to my board the way he used to, keeping us together. Out here on the water, it feels like we're outside of time. We lock eyes, and in the actual world, this would have felt uncomfortable after a while. But out on the water, Wyatt and I are both the past and the present. I am the girl who wasn't afraid of anything, all grown up without having been broken. I can feel the strength of that girl and I think he sees her. I don't want to look away.

"I'm going to take one more," he says finally, and lets go of my board. A wave comes and he glides right in. He seems to be able to feel the ocean beneath him and move along with its rhythm. It makes me think of our bodies together, and I push this thought away.

He's getting out of the ocean and I want to follow him.

My body is tired, but I take the next wave anyway. I'm not steady as I pop up, and then I am underwater, and I'm tumbling. My forehead scrapes something sharp in the sand and I wince in pain. *See? This is what happens.* My surfboard tugs at the leash on my ankle, and I'm too confused to stand up.

Wyatt grabs my arm and pulls me to standing. He quickly unleashes me from my board and puts his arms around me. I'm catching my breath as I lean into him, my head on his shoulder.

"You okay?" he asks, gathering my hair into a ponytail and wringing it out.

"I think so," I say. I don't want to get out of the ocean.

He pulls away and looks at me. "You're bleeding."

My hand flies up to my forehead, where I felt something sharp.

"Don't touch it. It's not that bad. Let me just rinse it with some salt water and cover it up. You okay to walk?"

"I'm fine, just disoriented from the water. Or reoriented. I don't know."

Wyatt grabs my board and takes my hand to lead me. "Please don't start talking crazy."

I laugh. I walk slowly because I'm a little dizzy, but also because I want to memorize this moment—the feel of Wyatt's hand in mine, the water at my ankles. The ocean floor is soft beneath my feet and the sun warms my back. My senses record every second of it.

Wyatt lays out our towels and shakes out his gray T-shirt. I sit down and he kneels over me, carefully folding the T-shirt and pressing it on my wound. His face is above mine and his bare chest fills my line of sight. I wonder why it's socially appropriate for people to wear so little when they are on the beach.

"I have no idea what I'm doing, by the way," he says.

"This all seems very professional to me."

He pulls the T-shirt away. "It's not too bad, the bleeding stopped." He sits back down on his towel, putting some space between us. We lean back on our elbows at the same time, stretching our legs out in front of us. It is shocking how undressed we are.

I say, "Have you ever thought about how much time we spent sitting together in our bathing suits growing up?"

"We lived at the beach."

"And we were half-naked all day. The two of us alone down at the cove all the time. I'm surprised it didn't happen a lot sooner."

Wyatt smiles at me. "It happened a lot sooner for me. I was just waiting for you to give me a sign."

"I gave you a million signs."

He looks back at the water. "I wanted to be sure. I had a lot to lose."

"I know." I have no idea why I brought this up. We're quiet now; all the lightness has been sucked back into the ocean.

"I'm really sorry I hurt you," he says finally.

I don't say anything.

"I think you can imagine what a mess I'd have to have been to walk away from what we had."

I sit all the way up so that I can fold into my knees. "I could have helped you."

"I would have pushed you away. I was reeling, and so angry with your family. I couldn't control it. The only thing worse than losing you would have been unleashing that on you."

I'm looking at my feet, which are getting sunburned. I scoop some sand over them.

"By the time my head cleared, you were so angry at me. And it was too late. Seems like such a waste."

"I don't know what to say."

"Say you forgive me."

"Of course I forgive you. It was forever ago. It doesn't matter."

Wyatt sits up and runs his hands through his hair. He looks away and then back at me. "It mattered, Sam. It may be over, but it mattered. So stop with that."

"I know." Of course I know.

He's quiet for a while. He looks at me and looks back at the water. "The way we felt that summer, it changed me. Like knowing that love could make a person that happy opened up something in me. It's why I can write songs. It gives me a lot of hope, that it's possible to feel that way. If what we had didn't matter, then my whole life is based on nothing."

I lower my forehead onto my knees and laugh a small laugh. If it was real, then nothing in my life since then makes sense.

"What?"

"Thinking it wasn't real, sort of acting like it was a dumb teenage obsession, was the only way I could get through it," I say.

He's quiet for a while. "We both turned out okay, right?"

I smile at Wyatt, who has turned out better than either of us ever imagined. I think of the trajectories we were on that summer, Wyatt with his laser focus on his music, and me just wanting to try everything. Wyatt's worked really hard to make his dream happen, and I've worked really hard to create a life that requires I try nothing.

"I might need to quit my job."

"For sure," he says. And we both lie down and take in the sun.

51

I can't sleep. I don't have any feeling of anxiety at all, more like excitement. I feel really good. It's that kind of good you feel when you've had the stomach flu and you wake up the next day and it's over. You forget how good it feels to be well. I spent practically the whole day outside. My muscles are the right kind of sore, and my skin feels alive from the sun. I try to think of how I can bring this feeling into my real life. I want to make room for surfing. I want to try things, wobble and fall down.

I look up at my tree of life, lit slightly by the moonlight. I don't like to critique my nine-year-old self, but it's a bit childish. One shade of brown for the trunk and all those branches. My dad was right, it needs texture. I rub my forefinger and thumb together to conjure the feeling of wood and remember the dead-tree museum in the dining room.

I get out of bed and knock on my parents' bedroom door. When there's no reply, I go in and tiptoe to my mom's side of the bed. I kneel down and put my hand on her arm. "Mom? Everything's okay."

"Why are you talking to me?"

"Do we have a glue gun?"

"Of course. Over the microwave."

"Can I have the sticks in that basket?"

"Of course," she says, and turns over.

I smile looking down at the two of them sleeping. The only two people in the world who would have absolutely no follow-up questions about why you might need a glue gun and sticks in the middle of the night.

BY SIX A.M. I am out of sticks, but most of the tree and its branches are covered. At first, I was gluing them to the wall in uniform lines, but as I went on I started placing them in a more organic way. I used to do things like this when I was a kid. I used to just follow myself into the night, into an idea that was going to either work or not. As I look at the wall now, I know that what I've created is not beautiful. It may even be a mess. But it's something.

I sleep for a few hours and find my mom at the kitchen table doodling and nursing a cup of coffee. "Wild night?" she asks me.

"I don't know what got into me. I just had to cover that tree in my room with texture. And your stick collection was exactly the thing."

"I can't wait to see it."

"You may need to burn the house down."

She laughs. "I don't want to hear that you're tired today, because there's a lot to do. I was going to start addressing these envelopes. You have an appointment at Ginnie's to taste the cake at one and then at the Old Sloop Inn to look at linens at two."

"Great," I say. "Wyatt said he'd come with me."

"How's your head?" she asks, and I misunderstand the question. I'm about to say it's clearing up, that I caught a glimpse of myself and I want to see more of her. I want to say that I'm afraid if I let her out she will fall madly in love with Wyatt and ruin my life. But she's looking at the Band-Aid on my forehead.

"Oh, it's fine," I say. She goes back to her doodling. I open the freezer and find a frozen peanut butter and jelly sandwich. I unwrap it and hold it, cold in my hand. I love that she's still buying these, waiting for her little girl to show up and eat them. "Mom, I'm sorry I've stayed away from the beach for so long."

She looks up at me and puts down her pen. "Me too. But I feel you coming back."

"Same," I say, and kiss the top of her head.

52

It feels funny walking down Main Street with Wyatt. In fourteen years, stores have turned over and lots of faces are new, but I can't shake the feeling that the town itself remembers us. The streetlights and the garbage cans, the red brick post office on whose steps we sat to watch the Fourth of July parade. I feel like we still look like a couple.

The bell over the door dings as we walk into Ginnie's Bakery. Ginnie's husband, Raoul, looks up from the cash register and puts his hand over his heart when he sees us. "I knew it!" he booms, stepping out from behind the counter. He hugs me and shakes Wyatt's hand. I know what's coming, and I know Wyatt knows too. He puts his arm around me to make sure it's coming. I think he thinks it's funny. I just can't.

"Hello," I say. "I see you remember Wyatt. He's here to help with the tasting. I'm marrying someone else."

Raoul's face falls. "Oh."

"Imagine how I feel," says Wyatt, and I give him a shove. Raoul quickly corrects himself. "I'm sorry, I just thought . . . You two walking in here the same way as when you were kids, the leaning. Ginnie always remarked about how you two walked together, sort of leaning into one another. We were like that too."

I am, I realize, sort of leaning toward Wyatt. I look at the space between our shoulders as we stand side by side and it's not normal. Wyatt is watching me notice this and gives me a shove back. "So let's talk cake," he says to Raoul.

"The cake. Yes, come sit down." We sit at a corner table where two slices of cake are waiting for us. Raoul introduces the first one. "This is a vanilla cake with a buttercream frosting with hints of lemon. Just hints."

We each take a bite. "It's delicious," I say.

"I'm not so sure," says Wyatt. "I taste no hints at all. What else have you got?"

"This is an outlandishly lemony cake with a lemon buttercream frosting. It's a bridal favorite."

We each take a bite and Wyatt nods. "It's outlandish all right."

I knock my knee into his. "Are there any more choices?"

"There's another one I like." Raoul goes back to the kitchen.

Wyatt's laughing as he reaches over to wipe frosting off my mouth with his napkin. He hasn't gotten it all, so he brushes the last bits of sugar with his fingers. I feel his fingers on my lips everywhere in my body. "You're a mess," he says.

Raoul brings us chocolate cake with vanilla frosting, layered with chocolate chip buttercream frosting. I must have made a sound when I tasted it.

"She likes this one," says Wyatt.

"You don't know that," I say.

"I know your sounds, Sam. She'll take this one."

"You can't have a chocolate cake for a wedding, right?"
I ask Raoul, taking a third bite.

"You can do whatever you want, but no, traditionally it's
white cake. The fun thing about this one is the white frosting looks traditional, and no one knows it's chocolate until
it's cut."

"Let's go back to the first two," I say.

"Sam, if you want a chocolate cake, get one. People love
chocolate cake, it's something no one can argue with."

"Jack won't like it," I say, and mop up the last chocolate
crumbs with my finger.

"You should have what you want." He's not joking
around anymore.

"I'll take the first one," I say.

WE WALK BACK up Main Street toward the Old Sloop
Inn, where we are supposed to be looking at linens for the
tables. I haven't slept and now I've eaten too much. "I'm
tired," I say. "Let's skip the linens and take naps."

"You're probably just going to pick white anyway," Wyatt says.

53

I nap hard. It's that narcotic kind of nap where you wake up sweaty and you don't know what time of day it is. My room is a forest now, and I lie flat on my back to take it in. I check my phone, and Jack's sent a photo from the US Open. I reply: Looks fun! I just had a long nap.

Jack: How was the cake?

Me: Delicious

Jack: What flavor did you choose?

Me: Vanilla

Jack: What about the linens?

Me: I haven't decided, I sort of liked the yellow

Jack: What were the other choices?

Me: All the colors, I'm going back tomorrow

Jack: Really, yellow?

Me: Probably white

I FIND MY dad on the back porch, drawing straight lines in his sketchbook. I take the lounge chair next to his and sort of wish it was time for cocktails.

"There's no life in a straight line," he says.

"Are you Confucius now?"

"Sounds like. My agent, who is very close to giving up on me, keeps telling me straight lines are selling. Horizontal gradations of color." He holds up his sketchbook to show me. "Does nothing for me." He turns to a new page and draws a straight line across the middle.

"Do you know much about wedding linens?" I ask him. He doesn't look up. "Not one thing."

"I kind of skipped going to the Old Sloop Inn today and lied to Jack about it. I can just go back tomorrow, right? They don't run out of them or anything?"

"It's a weird thing to lie about," he says. "Especially for a person who's so straight about everything." I'm looking at the water, but I can feel him looking right at me. He's been watching me ever since he drove Wyatt and me home that night. Like he's waiting to see what happens next.

His comment hangs in the air, inviting all the ugliness in. *Well you'd sure know about lying, Dad.* We're quiet for a minute.

"Cheating's just lying, but with your body," he says. I turn to him, and he's put down his sketch pad. I guess we're really going to do this.

"I'm not cheating. I lied about looking at linens."

"I think you lie to yourself a lot."

"Not true." I cross my arms over my chest to protect myself from this accusation.

"When I was having that thing with Marion, I was lying to your mom, but mostly just to support the lie I was telling myself." He meets my eye, as if to ask permission to continue. "People's interest, as you know, in my work was waning. All I was creating were flat versions of something that once worked. And one night Marion showed up here in this rainbow-striped dress and twirled in a way that sparked my imagination. For a second I stopped feeling old and washed up, like maybe I wasn't disappearing. It wasn't really about my work."

We're quiet. "Was it worth it?" I ask.

"Absolutely not. I was using Marion as a bridge to someplace else, someplace where I would feel like a different man. I was terrified that I wasn't good enough, but Marion wasn't going to fix me. I didn't become a new man, I just hurt everyone I loved."

I'm hugging my arms around my knees now, bracing for the rest. I have never wanted to have this conversation before, but I'm ready for it now. I turned my back on the whole mess with Wyatt, and I turned my back on myself, but ever since my dad sat in that car and witnessed Wyatt and me digging up what was lost, I feel like something's cracked open between us. I feel like he sees me, and I'm ready to see him.

"You cheat because you think it's going to make you someone else, that it's going to save you from your own damn misery. And that's the lie you're telling yourself. I guess that's the point, Sam. Another person is not going to turn you into anything but who you already are. Make sure you're not trying to turn yourself into someone else for Jack."

"I'm not," I say. "I mean I like having my act together."

"As long as it's not actually an act."

Guitar music comes from the treehouse and it occurs to me that I have never lied to Wyatt, not once.

"Speaking of liars, can you believe how sneaky Wyatt was about being a big shot?"

"I wasn't completely surprised."

And then I just ask it, because why the heck not. "Do you ever still think about her that way? Marion?"

"That's the weirdest part, Sam. Absolutely never. I can't even conjure up a memory of what I was feeling at the time, like it was temporary insanity. Getting caught was such a shock to my system that I had to take a hard look at my life. I don't lie to myself anymore. Or your mom."

"I really do want to live like that," I say. Then, in a practicing voice, I say, "I blew off looking at the napkins because I stayed up all night and then had a sugar crash."

"Was that so hard?"

54

"My goodness! The bounty!" my mother says that night as Wyatt walks up the back porch, clutching three bottles of wine to his chest. My dad, Travis, and Hugh are all sitting around a big platter of cheeses and meats outside. I smile at the sight of them all together. Maybe this is possible, this whole impossible group. It's my life plus Wyatt, which I have to admit feels more like my actual life. Just seeing Wyatt standing there practically within reaching distance makes me feel like everything is going to be okay.

"Maybe stick this in the fridge," he says, handing me a bottle of Chablis.

I look at the label and back at him. "This feels awfully grown-up. Is this something we do now?"

"Yes. I also file a tax return." He looks over my shoulder and says hello to Travis.

"Did you nap?" I ask.

"Like the dead," he says.

"Can we go surfing tomorrow?" I ask.

"I don't know. Was surfing on your wedding checklist for this weekend?"

"Right," I say. "Linens and flowers."

We turn to see Gracie walking home through the dunes with Andy Bryant from two doors down. They're both carrying surfboards so it's a tight squeeze. He says something to her and she lowers her head and looks away so he doesn't see her smile.

"Did you see that?" I ask.

"I did," Wyatt says. "That kid should run for his life."

I want to laugh, but it doesn't feel like Wyatt's kidding around anymore. It feels like he's pulling away. It's subtle, but Wyatt's pulling away is imprinted in all of my cells, like my body remembers.

WHEN CHICKEN AND corn are served, my dad makes a toast. "To old friends," he says. "And to summer's end."

Gracie moans. "School starts Tuesday. Two more days at the beach and then it's over."

"Ugh," I say, and everyone looks at me for an explanation. "It's just that I'm on this mind-numbing assignment where I'm trapped in my cubicle all day making charts that prove there's really nothing we can do to improve the client's situation."

"That sounds like hell," my dad says.

"Your life is my worst nightmare," says Travis, gesturing with an ear of corn.

"Maybe you can use your extra brainpower to focus on

the wedding," says Hugh. "Wouldn't be the worst thing in the world for you to have a little extra time over the next month."

"True," says my mom.

Wyatt's quiet, and he won't meet my eye. He asks my mom, "Is there a lot to do?"

She laughs. "To put a wedding together in eight weeks? I'd say."

"I swear I'll actually go to the florist tomorrow," I say.

Wyatt still won't look at me. My mom says, "And we're going to have to get these invitations in the mail next week. Maybe you can come over Tuesday night and we can get them all assembled and stamped."

"I like the painted ones," says Gracie. "I think we should glue little shells to the bottom corner."

"And maybe even a little sand," my mom says.

"Mom," I say.

"I know, sorry. I can't help myself," my mom says. She pours everyone some more wine.

Gracie gets up from the table and runs inside to get a few of the painted invitations to pass around. I get one with a pale yellow swoosh of color and I finger the corner where there really should be seashells. I pass it across the table to Wyatt.

He takes the card from me and holds it with both hands. He runs his thumb along the yellow, over our names. I'm trying to read his face, because in a way he seems surprised, like maybe he didn't expect Jack's and my names to be there. I want him to look up at me, but he's just staring at that card.

Gracie says, "What do you think? Better with the color, right?"

He says, "Much."

"I'm telling you Jack would never go for it," I say. "So don't get too attached."

Wyatt finally meets my eye and shakes his head. He gets up from the table and answers his phone, which I did not hear ring. When he's back, he doesn't look right.

"I have to get going. Like back to LA," he says.

"Did something happen?" my mom asks.

"Yes. It's fine, but Missy's on a tighter deadline than we thought to record her new album." Wyatt looks at me, and then at my engagement ring. I haven't noticed him do that before. "Anyway, I'm going to see about a flight and all that. Thank you for dinner." Everyone is on their feet to say goodbye. He hugs Gracie and tells her to knock their socks off in eighth grade. He hugs Hugh and then Travis.

My dad hugs him too. "Well, son, now that we know you're rich and famous, we're going to have to come see you in California. Maybe do a little Rollerblading."

"Oh, God help us," says my mom.

"That would be great. Michael would love that too."

He turns to me and I grab both of his hands. "I wish you were staying," I say. "This really feels like the last night of summer now, and I hate the last night of summer."

"I know," he says. "See you, Sam." He walks down the porch steps into the dunes, and everyone sits back down and carries on with their conversations. This isn't right. Hours ago we were laughing and tasting cake. Hours ago there was no space between us.

I'm on my feet and running down the steps to the dunes. I have not thought through how my family is going to perceive this, but I don't really care. I can't let Wyatt leave this way.

I catch up to him as he's about to walk through the sliding glass door into his house.

"Hey, what's going on?" I say.

He turns and sees me and actually looks annoyed that I'm there. Wyatt has been happy to see me my entire life.

"I've got to get out of here," he says.

"Why? I thought you were staying the weekend and we were going to do stuff tomorrow."

He seems agitated and is looking over my shoulder at the dunes. "You know what it is, Sam? I hate your cake. Your cake sucks."

I smile because this must be a joke. "My cake sucks?"

It's no joke. "Yes, it's boring and you don't like it that much. But you're going to choose it because you think it's the right cake for this life you've buried yourself in. And Jack just lets you disappear, maybe because he doesn't care or maybe because he doesn't even know who you are. If it were me—and it was me, so I know—I'd want you to be everything you could be. I wouldn't be putting rules and constraints around you, I'd just love you and let you move through the world the way you wanted to. You've just given up, Sam. You're hiding, and it's pathetic."

"That's so mean." The words are so quiet coming out of my mouth, like it's my last breath.

"Well it's true. And I can't believe no one else has called you out on it. What the hell is wrong with your family? I can't believe your dad thinks you're being honest with your-self here."

He doesn't, I don't say.

"You're the cake that looks normal until people dig in and find out it's spectacular. You're the chocolate fucking cake, Sam, and you won't even choose it."

I'm looking up at his face, and I see something that looks like disgust. I reach out to take his hands in mine, and he puts them in his back pockets. "You're angry at me because I didn't pick the chocolate cake."

"You're the most important person that's ever been in my life, and you're not even the most important person in your own."

"That's not true," I say. I reach out and rest my hand on his forearm.

He grabs that hand. "And this, Sam. You're touching me all the time. Do you run your hands over all your other friends this way? You don't know what you want or who you are. You're gasping for air."

I have nothing to say. I'm embarrassed about my rogue hands. I am hurt that he thinks my life is such a fake joke. I want to be angry, because anger would help me storm off back to the safety of my own house. My kingdom for a little righteous indignation right now. I just look straight ahead at his chest.

"I'm going to bed," he says. "And I'm leaving tomorrow. Get your shit together, Sam."

55

My shit together. Mine? I'm in bed when the anger finally shows up. I'm the one who's in a healthy relationship. Wyatt's just been occasionally sleeping with a pop star. And maybe I'm not showing my full colors and chasing my dreams, but it's not like he's up on a stage performing either. If he thinks I'm hiding behind Jack, what does he call feeding Missy songs and letting her wreck them? Ha! Who's really lost their voice here?

I have a text from Jack at midnight: Miss you!!!

I stare at it in the dark. Why all the exclamation points? I hold my finger over them to read it as simply: Miss you. The quiet "miss you" is so much more romantic, like he's got his head on the pillow, texting me because he misses me. The shouting text makes me feel like he's in a bar and just remembered he owed me a high five.

Am I now such a tight-ass, I wonder, that I am editing my fiancé's texts? I write back: Miss you too.

I SLEEP UNTIL eight, presumably because I have a sleep debt, and find my mom at the dining room table, deep into her watercolors. She doesn't look up when she says, "What happened with Wyatt?"

I pour myself a coffee and examine the row of invitations on the counter.

"We broke up again."

"Sam." She puts down her paintbrush.

"He laid into me about all this stuff. It started with my wedding cake, he thinks he knows which one I like best. And then it spun out of control to his accusing me of living a total lie."

"Oh."

"What? Do you think I'm living a lie?"

"I think you've constructed a really nice life that you feel safe in."

"What's wrong with safe?"

"Nothing at all. Safe is great. There's just a balance between safe and free, and I think you're a person who might like to be a little more free in your life than you are."

"I'm too old to run around playing Capture the Flag, Mom."

"Not necessarily. But you could speak up a little more in your relationship. Jack loves you, and I bet he'd love you even more if he saw more of you."

I pick up an invitation that has a pale blue brushstroke across our names and the lightest orange dots at the corners. *Happy,* I think. I like the idea of a wedding that begins with an invitation that doesn't mind a pop of color. They are such small touches but they put me in our wedding, or at least something that feels like me.

"They're beautiful, Mom. They give this whole thing a burst of happy energy."

She looks up and smiles at me. "Good. That's what we needed." She goes back to her work and adds, "How could Jack turn down a burst of happy energy?"

56

The waves are okay in front of our house, and Gracie and I surf until lunchtime. I'm happy to be spending the morning with Gracie doing something where we don't have to talk. The lights are out in Wyatt's house, so I assume he's left. I'm ruminating on our last conversation in a way that's probably not healthy. I can't believe Wyatt called me a liar and a fraud, or whatever. But mostly I can't believe he called me out on wanting to touch him all the time. I'm embarrassed thinking about it, like the disconnect between what my body wants and what my mind knows to be appropriate is evident to everyone around me.

Gracie comes with me to the Old Sloop Inn and we actually choose the yellow napkins. She tells me my whole wedding is going to look like sunshine. I think of the water-colored invitations and imagine a yellow ribbon around my waist. I breathe a little easier having made these small decisions, as if for the first time I can picture myself being part of this day and smiling a real smile into a camera.

By the time we've finished dinner, Wyatt should have

landed in Los Angeles. He hasn't texted me all day, which is expected. His last piece of advice was for me to get my shit together, so I can't really imagine what his follow-up would be. He's disappointed in how I've turned out, which is his problem, not mine.

I STAY AT the beach until Monday to help close up the house. I wake up with an anxious heart. We're packing to leave, summer's over, and things are off with Wyatt. I check my phone. It's six a.m.; no text. This is a decade-old feeling that I'm walking through, and I need to shake it off. I get up and put on a bathing suit and run out through the dunes into the ocean. It's cold but I've been swimming enough times over the past few days that my body is used to it. I dive under the waves and then swim toward the cove with slow, even strokes. No one's going to be up for an hour, I can be out here as long as I like.

My mind relaxes in the water, like my body takes over and I can just enjoy the rhythm of the movement. It reminds me of being a kid, when I spent the whole day just sort of seeking out what felt good. What feels good right now is a wedding with a burst of sunshine. I'm going to wear my hair loose and feel like myself. I have a nagging feeling about what Wyatt said about Jack's not really knowing me. If Jack doesn't have a complete picture of who I am, that's my own fault.

When I get to the cove I walk straight to the linden tree. It's littered with seaweed and shells that actually look as if they washed up on a single wave. How pointless it was to have spent so much time and energy organizing my shells to look the way nature would have arranged them anyway. It was pointless and fun and satisfying, actually. Like a flash mob. I choose a particularly pretty green and blue shell from the mess, tuck it in the side of my bathing suit, and swim back home.

I ride back to the city with my parents and Gracie. We pass through town and drive onto Sunrise Highway, onto the Long Island Expressway, and through the tunnel. It's transformative, this ride. We leave the beach behind and wake up to the excitement of the city.

They drop me off in front of my building and I squeeze Gracie extra tight. "I'll see you tomorrow night to stuff envelopes," I say. "Good luck tomorrow!"

Jack and I decide to go to our favorite neighborhood Italian restaurant. He's gotten a little bit of sun at the US Open and looks handsomer than ever, but I don't mention it.

When we're seated with two glasses of red wine and two plates of spaghetti, he asks, "So do you think we'll be able to pull this off in eight weeks?"

"No problem," I say. "We just have to make a few final decisions this week, get the invitations in the mail, and then we're all set."

"Okay, shoot. What are the decisions?" He leans back in his chair and crosses his arms. I like how with Jack I feel like we are running our life like it's a small company. We talk through options, make solid decisions, and move on.

"Linens. Gracie and I like yellow napkins on white tablecloths. My mom will have the florist come up with something that goes with that. That little pop of color makes the whole room feel like sunshine. You'll love it." *You'll love it* is a bit much. It comes out as a command, which isn't like me. "I mean I think you will. What do you think?" I lean forward and take his hand, which is awkward for some reason.

"I don't know, Sam. We kind of talked about white for the whole wedding. Classic, right?"

"Yeah, but the color really feels happy."

"It's a wedding, isn't it already happy?"

"Very," I say, and squeeze his hand. I don't know why I feel like I'm in a sales situation, like I'm trying to coax a stranger into buying a rug.

"Well, I'm not sure," he says. "What else? You decided on the cake?"

I take a sip of my wine and lean back in my chair. The cake is a sore subject now that it's been used to lambast my entire life. "Yes, the vanilla."

"Okay, good." Jack's twirling his spaghetti around his fork, and I have the feeling he thinks this conversation is over. It's not.

"There's one more thing I wanted to talk about." I reach into my bag and pull out one of our invitations. This one has a pale blue swoosh over our names, and it feels like the flow of the ocean. I hand it to him.

"Ah, I see your mom's been busy. Were there extras?"

"About twenty."

"Cute." He puts it down and goes back to his spaghetti.

"I really love it," I say.

"What?"

"The invitation with the paint across our names. My

mom did them in a bunch of different colors. I actually love all of them."

"Sam, it's a cute idea but there's no way. We agreed on the invitations because we wanted something monochrome. What did the stationery lady call it? 'Traditional tones'?"

"Maybe we need to move beyond monochrome." There's too much weight to my words. I wanted to say it lightly, like with a question mark at the end. But it comes out like a declaration, which I guess is how I mean it. I really need some color in my life.

"Oh God, Sam. You've spent too much time this summer with your parents." He laughs at this and goes back to his spaghetti.

I look down at my plate and try to manage the anger that's creeping up. I don't like his tone about my parents, and I actually want to spend more time out there, not less. "It was good for me, I think, being out there more than once this summer. It's nice, how they sort of get loose. They're happy."

"They probably are, but it's a little nuts. Like they're kids." He holds up the invitation for emphasis.

"They're artists, not kids." We're quiet for a second. Jack eats his spaghetti and I watch. Finally I say, "When I was a kid in the summer I used to wake up in the morning and just follow the day wherever it took me. I didn't wear shoes, ever. I just moved in and out of the ocean, making up games and digging in the sand." There, that's who I am.

Jack smiles at my memory. "Idyllic," he says. "But you can't keep doing that the rest of your life." He gestures with his fork. "Our kids are going to take tennis lessons."

Tennis lessons. There is absolutely nothing wrong with tennis lessons. I picture little children in clean white clothes with little white sneakers, double tied, learning to hit the ball within the confines of that rectangle. Over and over again. It feels like waltzing as I see it in my mind.

IT'S NINETY-FIVE DEGREES outside, but I'm wearing a sweater in my cubicle. Everything feels unnatural. It's the day after Labor Day and it feels like the first day back at school, everyone seated in straight lines and in hard shoes. Eleanor has a new assignment for me. I'm hoping it's in Central Park.

"Come in," she says, lowering her reading glasses. "How was the weekend?"

"Good."

"Wedding plans coming along?"

"Sort of."

"Good. Now, I have a new assignment for you once you've finished up that health care thing. It's perfect because it can all be done from here, just you and the data." Scold me, punish me, but do it once. I do not need her to keep bringing this up.

"What's the assignment?"

"An insurance company wants to unload twenty percent of its sales force. They have sales data and time logs, you just need to identify who needs to go. They'd like to fire them on Friday, so maybe get started this afternoon." Ah, the old Friday firing. She hands me a file.

"Are you cold in here?" I ask.

"No."

It's crazy that we'd have to open a window to warm up. Crazier still that the windows don't open. I'm pacing the tiny space between the guest chairs and her desk.

"Are you sick?" Eleanor asks.

It's a great question, really. I check in with my body. My chest feels tight and my lungs don't seem to be able to take in a full breath. I try to remember the signs of a woman having a heart attack.

"I'm fine, I think. I just, I don't know. I need some air." I turn to leave.

"Fine, get some air, but we need this midday Friday," she says. And I can't quite imagine it, not one more minute of sitting in that cubicle making decisions about people I don't know based on random criteria. Making a spreadsheet and sorting it high to low and then sending a wrecking ball into the bottom twenty percent's lives, no questions asked. This isn't who I want to be anymore, and it's certainly not who I am. Before I know it, I am in bare feet with my good work shoes in my hands. My body has decided.

"Thank you, Eleanor, for everything you've done for me, but I really need to get out of here. I'm not coming back."

I STEP OUT of the building with eyes closed because I want to feel the heat of the day on my skin. I changed into the flip-flops I kept in my desk for lunchtime pedicures and left my work shoes in their place. It's a decision I'll probably regret, but walking away from them right now feels great. I walk into the park, and the old oaks on the Poet's Walk applaud me with their darkest green leaves. I am so relieved and joyful, as if I've just gotten some great news. I sit down on a bench to text Jack. I can't quite get the words out: I quit my job. I should tell him in person tonight. I can't text Wyatt. I don't feel like engaging with my parents. I text Travis: I quit my job.

Travis: Nervous breakdown?

Me: The opposite

JACK COMES BACK from Tuesday night tennis and doesn't notice that I've made dinner until after his shower. "What's all this?" He kisses me and grabs a spear of asparagus off the baking sheet.

"I'm celebrating, I think."

"What? Did you send out the invitations? I thought that was tomorrow night."

That was actually tonight, I think. I totally forgot. "I quit my job."

He puts down the end of his asparagus. "Wait. Why?"

"I hate it. I mean it was tolerable when I got to go to different companies and sort of engage with people, but now that I'm stuck in my cubicle with reams of paper, I just can't handle it."

He walks out of the kitchen and starts pacing in the living room, like he needs more space to process this. I have a horrible feeling that I've made a mistake, that I've pulled the rug out from under myself. "Lots of people hate their jobs sometimes, Sam. I just had a full day of adult acne. I didn't quit."

I'm not sure what I was thinking. I was so excited walking by the Fresh Market and picking up food for dinner. I think I sort of thought he might be excited that I was getting out of a rut.

"I felt like I couldn't breathe," I say.

"Then you go home sick. Or you take a walk. You don't quit. And maybe we could have talked about this."

"Let's talk about it now." I sit down on the couch and wait for him to sit next to me. "I think maybe that whole flash mob thing was a cry for help, or even the last gasp of the real me because she was about to disappear forever. I can't spend the rest of my life keeping strangers in line."

Jack puts his arms around me and I fall into his hug. This is what I was hoping for, that Jack would understand and want me to do whatever I need to do to be happy.

"Okay," he says. "It's going to be okay. Eleanor has invested a lot of time in you. I say you just call her tonight and come clean. You've been under a lot of stress with the wedding, but of course you want to keep your job."

I pull out of the hug. "Did you hear what I said? I'm not going back to that job."

He takes my hands. "Of course you are. You're good at it. You're well paid. You'll probably hate your next job too sometimes, that's what work is."

I do not communicate with Jack. I don't know why I'm just realizing this now. I toss my words over to him and they hit a wall and slide to the ground. There's no give-and-take, no discussion. "I tried to tell you I want to teach art."

"Well that's irrational."

"What's irrational about teaching?"

He's exasperated and lets out a dramatic breath. "You don't have a degree in education, you have no experience, you'll make less money than you're making now. Want more?"

I am strangely emboldened by his rigidity. Like I want to throw more ideas at him and watch them bounce off, just to prove how rigid he is. "Is there anything that you'd support me doing that is outside of the scope of your life plan?"

"It's our life plan, Sam. Two kids three years apart, starting in three years. All the stuff we've been over."

"What about three kids, two years apart?"

"That's too many kids," he says, like it's a fact he just read in the *Encyclopedia of Family Planning*. "It's too much tuition."

"Plus all those tennis lessons," I say.

He relaxes. "Yes, exactly."

I'm relaxed too. I've loosened my grip on this thing I've been holding on to and I'm so close to letting it go. I consider tossing him one more, maybe asking what he thinks about a chocolate wedding cake, but I know. I've known for a long time. Jack has no idea who I am, and I don't think he wants to know.

Jack is leaning back on the couch, satisfied that he's made his point and that I'm going to fall in line. Falling in line has been my signature move my whole adult life. I want to lean over and mess up his hair. I want to replace all of this furniture with—I don't know what; I've never even picked out furniture. I run my hand over the gray tweed of the sofa, and I look up at his handsome face. This isn't his fault.

He's been up-front about who he is and what he wants from the very first day. I'm the one who's been lying and with-holding herself.

I take off my ring and hand it to him. "I can't do this, Jack."

57

I arrive at my parents' apartment unannounced. I hug my dad with both arms and stay in that hug longer than I have in years. He's not very surprised to hear that I've quit my entire life in one day. We sit at the dining room table and my mom keeps asking if I'm okay, hungry, thirsty, sleepy.

My dad knows I'm fine. "Sometimes you have to walk away from all the things you don't want to make room for the future. Blank canvas."

"Yes," I say, and Gracie reaches over and takes my hand. She doesn't say a word, but I feel the hope that she's given me her entire life. My dad puts his arm around my mom.

I did the right thing, I know it. But I'm exhausted. Breaking out of a life that's not working is a lot of work. It might have been easier to have kept doing what I was doing for the next fifty years.

I smile at Gracie. "Should I get unpacked? It's been a long time since we've had a sleepover here." We walk into her room, and I throw my bag on the bottom bunk.

"Oh," she starts. "That's where I sleep." I am feeling just

how small this room is. I don't know how Travis and I ever lived here together.

"That's fine," I say, moving my bag to the top bunk. "I like it up there too." Gracie's looking at me, like she's waiting to see what I'm going to do next.

Her phone is pinging, and she looks at it and laughs. She types something in response and laughs. She looks up and seems surprised to see me still standing there. "Sorry, I'm just going to . . . My friend is calling. So."

"Oh my God. Sorry," I say. Gracie doesn't want me here. Gracie is growing up and wants her privacy, and here I was hoping we were going to play safari and eat Twizzlers. Oh my God. I back out of the room and find my mom in the kitchen drying dishes.

"Do you think there's any person on this earth who is more of a loser than I am?" I grab a towel and start drying. "Be honest, can you name one person?"

"You're not a loser, Sam."

"Really," I say. "Let's review the facts. I'll be thirty-one this month. I have no job and no relationship. And," I say, holding up the salad tongs for emphasis, "my twelve-year-old sister is too cool for me."

My mom laughs, sort of. "It's not so bad, Sam. You have your education and you can start again. And I'm pretty sure you weren't dreaming of being Gracie's roommate forever."

"The last time my life was in free fall, she really helped."

My mom places a stack of plates on the counter. "Are you in free fall?"

"What do you mean?"

"I mean I've been watching you, like for signs that you're not going to be okay. And you seem okay, but I don't know. Maybe I can't tell anymore."

I take her in my arms, and her head is heavy on my shoulder. "Mom, I quit a job I didn't like and left a man I didn't want to marry. I just need to regroup and figure out what I do like. I'll be fine." This feels good to say, like I am capable of being my own parent. "You don't need to worry about me."

THAT NIGHT, ON the top bunk, I get a text from Wyatt: I heard. You okay?

I stare at the phone for a bit, letting an odd combination of relief and fear wash over me.

Me: Well I'm single, jobless and homeless. So not sure

Wyatt: Did you do the right thing?

Me: Yes

Wyatt: I'm sorry I left like that. It was just all too much. I don't know why I thought it would be fun to come out and help you get married

Me: Weren't you already coming?

Wyatt: No. I wanted to see you, so I came. Honestly don't know what I was thinking

My heart rate picks up and I strain my eyes in the dark to make sure I've read that correctly. He just wanted to see me. Lying in this bed and looking at that same crack in the ceiling that I studied for a year while waiting for Wyatt to call, I feel afraid. I have just made the first step toward getting reacquainted with myself, and I am terrified of opening up to the tidal wave that is Wyatt. And yet.

Me: You could come back

I wait an eternity for his reply.

Wyatt: I can't. I have to be here for Missy's new album and I kind of hate how it's coming together. Like the more famous she gets, the more she ad libs and the songs feel wrong

It feels too easy, the way he's changed the subject. Like he's dodged my saying I want him to come.

Me: Maybe you should write for someone else

Wyatt: Carlyle would probably kill me. Anyway, glad you made a decision. Let me know if you need anything?

Sam: I'm definitely going to need a friend

I'd rather have Wyatt as a friend than not have him in my life at all, but it's a half-truth. I'd say more, but I don't want him to change the subject again.

Wyatt: Deal. Good night, Sam-I-am.

He's gone, and I am smiling at the phone. He could have just said good night.

I RIDE THE elevator up to what is now Jack's apartment. There's a gravity to what I'm doing, plus it also feels like breaking and entering. Jack knows I'm coming. I told him I'd use my key and then leave it with the doorman. He'll be home in ninety minutes, which is plenty of time for me to pack up my stuff and be gone. When I get to the fourteenth floor, I walk more quickly than normal to the apartment door. I don't want to see my neighbors. I don't want to explain why I decided not to marry this perfect man. My family seems to totally understand. But people who know me less well, the ones who think I've got my act together, will think I'm making a horrible mistake, like I'm the girl in the horror movie who is running further into the house.

The key turns easily. I've brought two duffel bags with me and fill them quickly with my clothes. I fill a box with the stuff from my desk and a few framed photos of my family. I open and close the kitchen cabinets. Jack paid for all of that stuff, and I wouldn't have any place to put it anyway. I stand there for a minute looking at my bags. I'm doing mental gymnastics thinking of how I could unpack them into a dresser that does not exist in a corner of Gracie's room that is already occupied. I don't know how I've moved so far backward in my life that I am sharing a room with Gracie, and I don't know how I ever got so far from having a life that feels like mine. I look around this gray, gray room and I start to cry.

I don't want this. I am sure of it. I say it out loud. I've been bowling with the bumpers up. Talk about pointless. I need space to regroup, and I need time in the ocean. I lug my stuff to the elevator and catch a cab to Penn Station.

58

Long Island is a great idea. The first night I'm there I eat popcorn for dinner and sit on the deck watching the waves reach their foamy hands out to me and invite me in. It's still summer-warm but hazy, and the moonlight is diffused over the water. The limitlessness of the ocean beyond the horizon exhilarates me. I can't see what's just past that line, and if I swam out to it, there would be another line I wouldn't be able to see past. I just know that what's ahead of me is the rest of my life, starting with tonight. And then tomorrow.

There's a light, constant breeze off the water that tickles my skin and makes me think of Wyatt. I'm confusing the feel of the breeze with the feel of his skin on mine. There was a time, of course, when these sensations would happen at once, the breeze skimming Wyatt's hands on my skin. If I'm going to stay out here, I am going to have to get used to feeling him in the air, hearing him in the sound of the gulls. Now that I'm listening to my heart, I realize he's been right there all along anyway.

On my second night, I decide I need to do something

about my bedroom. I start picking the sticks off my tree of life. Maybe now that my life is such a sticky art project, my room doesn't need to be. When I've put them all back in my mom's stick-collecting basket, I step back to take in what is now a poorly painted tree dotted with dried glue. The ugliness of it starts to close in on me and I open my window. The moon is low over the water and the salty night air blows in. *More of this*, I think. I grab a sweater and head out the back door, through the dunes, and up the rope ladder to the treehouse. Wyatt's guitars are gone, and his rug has a few leaves on it, but the futon is still there with a painter's tarp thrown over it for protection. I pull off the tarp and lie down on the futon, remembering what it felt like to be there with Wyatt, just talking, talking, talking. The next night I go back to the treehouse with sheets, a blanket, and candles.

I secure a part-time job working for Mrs. Barton fifteen hours per week running a reading enrichment program after school. It'll be enough to cover my food bill. I should be padding my résumé and my bank account and angling for the next big thing. But it feels great not to. The thing about my old job was that there was no collaboration, no back-and-forth. I came in with the plan and that was that. In this life, working with kids, it's like I'm offering an idea and they're offering one back. We follow those ideas around until it's time to go home. I wonder if this was my dream all along.

When I hear from Wyatt, it's always late at night. If he calls and I'm in the treehouse, it's an extra thrill. Sometimes I'm asleep and he's on his deck watching the sunset. I always wake up to respond. I think a lot about what Dr.

Judy would say. If I'm addicted to Wyatt, there's no way this counts as sober.

Wyatt: Are you up?

Me: Why are you up? It's even late there

Wyatt: Having a rough day. Wondered how your day was

I stretch out on the futon and take in the totally luxurious feeling of knowing he's waiting for my response. Dr. Judy would flip.

Me: It was maybe my best day. We read a story about dragons, and I had construction paper and scissors for us to all make our own dragon. But this kid Miranda, like six years old, says dragon is like drag on. She takes her chair and drags it on the carpet to make her point. And I'm like wow this is phonics or something so we spend the whole rest of the afternoon dragging each other on chairs. And I did not get fired

Wyatt: I think you've found your calling

Me: What was so rough about your day?

Wyatt: I tried to quit my job and found out I can't

Me: What does that mean

Wyatt: I tried to tell Carlyle I don't want to write for Missy anymore, that I want to try writing that movie or just try something else. I can't stand handing her a song and having her turn it into crap. He said he stands to make $100 million off her next album and if I don't finish it he'll ruin me

Me: He can't do that

Wyatt: He actually can. He has a lot of power out here

Me: That's horrible

Wyatt: So I guess I'm going to wake up tomorrow and write Missy another song

I don't know how to reply. I'm going to wake up tomorrow and go for a swim. I want to tell Wyatt to walk away from that mess and meet me at the beach. Which is selfish and absurd. I'm lying in a treehouse with nothing to lose, and he's fighting to reclaim his creative independence. I'm not going to walk outside tomorrow and find him sitting on the back porch waiting for me. I'm not going to wake up in the middle of the night and feel his breath on my neck. A breeze comes in from the water and moves over me like Wyatt himself. I think of the least desperate thing I can type.

Me: I bet it will be a great song

Wyatt: Tell me about the kids at the library

As I text him the highlights of my day, I can picture him looking out at the beach that's facing the wrong way. He's in a really bad place again, and I'm glad that I'm here for him this time. When we've said good night, I close my eyes and picture Wyatt the way I want to see him, happy, with his guitar in his hands, and I let the waves sing me back to sleep.

59

I've been in Long Island for a week, and I've started getting up to swim in the ocean first thing, even before my coffee. I'm trying to swim half a mile down the beach and back, and I'm getting close, depending on the tides. I remember the days of counting my laps in the YMCA pool, in a constant negotiation with God. Stripped down now, I'm just me in the water, swimming stroke after stroke because I want to, because it feels good. When it stops feeling good, I will stop.

That night under my blanket on the futon I text him: New best day today

He doesn't text me back, and I lie there wondering what he could be doing and who he's with. I have an idea of what his life in LA looks like, what his view is. I imagine him in dark-colored sheets, and I don't know why. I fall asleep picturing Wyatt in dark-colored sheets.

Hours later a text wakes me: Tell me

I blink and stretch, then reply: It's the middle of the night, you have no boundaries

Wyatt: I didn't know we had any, I think I wrote a song about this

This makes me smile, and I pull the covers up over us.

Me: So it was pirate day and I had these swashbuckling costumes so that we could perform a ten-minute play. But they hated my play and wrote their own—in three acts—to perform for me.

Wyatt: How was it

Me: Nonsense and violent. Can't wait till tomorrow, reading a book about soup. Who knows?

Wyatt: That's the best thing ever. Go back to sleep

AS EXPECTED, THE whole soup thing doesn't go as expected. I brought soup for tasting, and instead, the kids wanted to peel off the labels and make a collage. I ride my bike home with a basket full of unmarked cans that will get me through a dozen surprise dinners. This feels like my whole life right now, knowing generally where I'm going without a single specific spelled out for me. I honestly don't care what kind of soup I eat.

I pull into my driveway and choose one can of soup to bring inside. It's warm for mid-September, and the wisteria has lost its blooms but not its leaves. I run one between my fingers and feel that dark-green-turning-to-brown feel.

After dinner (chicken noodle!), I take a beer up to the treehouse to watch the sunset. It's a great place to sketch, and I've finished three different takes on Gracie walking through the dunes with that Bryant kid. I'm trying to capture that in-between stage where she's just figured out why she should be a little self-conscious. I wonder if I'm in an in-between stage where I'm figuring out why I shouldn't.

I decide my drawing of Gracie is nearly finished. I turn to a new page and start to sketch Wyatt, sitting on a stool, singing at the Owl Barn. I am concentrating on the way the fabric of his shirt lies on his shoulders. I reach for my phone to text him but decide to wait. It's only four thirty in Los Angeles, and I'd rather be talking to him when he's lying down.

60

Wyatt

I leave my suitcase and my guitar on the front steps, because I don't want to wait any longer. It was a long trip, but then again, it's been a long decade. Her bike's out front with a bunch of unlabeled cans in the basket. This is so random, and it makes me smile. I know there's a story behind it. I knock on her door, and there's no response.

The sun's setting, and she could be on the beach. I walk around her porch and down the back steps and through the dunes. There's no one on the beach. I have this horrible feeling that I've missed her, that there was this tiny window of time where I could have had her back, but I missed it, and she's gone to Europe or met someone else. I shake off this thought; I just talked to her yesterday.

I could have told her over the phone. I wanted to, but I also wanted to see her face, to know for sure if she was all in with me. I didn't want to lay it all out there and then sit on an airplane second-guessing her response. I hurt her worse than I ever imagined, and I need to see her to know if she's going to be able to trust me again. After all, she left Jack, but she didn't leave him for me.

I walk back through the dunes and into my own yard, and I see legs dangling off the side of the treehouse. They are my favorite legs. I want to rush over and climb up that ladder, but I stop myself for a second just to look. She's drawing, and she's completely in her head. Her hair is a mess, like she went for a long swim this morning and just let it dry in the sun. That's the rest of my life, right there. I am a little afraid of how happy I feel as I walk over to the rope ladder. The last time I was this happy, I lost everything.

"Hey, Sam-I-am."

She looks up and her eyes go wide. "Wyatt." She puts down her pad and pencil and stands up as I'm climbing the ladder. She throws her arms around me and hugs me tight. I pull her even closer and feel the front of her body touch every part of mine. My thumbs loop themselves into the waistline of her jean shorts, just like they always did. I am back in time and also not; we aren't the same people we were. I can't believe I've traveled so far in my hunt for a happy life, and my happy life is right here, in my treehouse. "Were you going to tell me you were here?" she asks.

"I'm telling you now." I breathe in the salty smell of her hair as her head rests heavy on my shoulder. There's something about Sam pressed against me that floods me with relief, like I was about to fade away but I've been restored to my full strength. I want to run my hands under her T-shirt and rest them on the small of her back. I want to kiss that spot on her neck and hear her catch her breath the way I've always remembered.

"What are you doing here?" She peels her head off my shoulder and looks me in the eye. She has a little bit of sand in her eyebrow and I wonder if it's been there all day. "Is everything okay?"

"Yes, I think so," I say.

"What does that mean?" She takes my hands and examines my fingers. She runs her hands over the back of them and then the front. This is the first time we've been together as two single adults, and there's no reason to tell her to stop touching me. I could stand here all day just feeling the feather touch of her hands skimming mine, but I have to say what I came to say.

"I ran away from Los Angeles."

"Like you quit your job?"

"I quit Carlyle, and I quit Missy."

"This sounds like a long story." I search her eyes for any sign that she's disappointed that I've given that up. But all I see there is happiness, as if anything I tell her is going to be okay. The way Sam is looking at me reminds me of how I felt that last summer—that I was good enough in my own right because I was good enough for her. She leads me over to the futon. "I can't believe you're here."

There's a sheet and a blanket on the futon, a lit candle on the little table, and a pair of white slippers on the floor. I smile because it feels like Sam's been waiting for me. This may have been what I imagined as a kid, living in this tree-house with Sam, her slippers on the floor. "Looks like you've moved in," I say.

"I like it here," she says, and we both sit down. She drapes her legs over mine in a way that is so familiar to both of us that I can't help but put my arm around her. She rests her head in the crook of my neck and I'm trying to remember where I was going to start with this story.

61

I can't believe he's here.

He rests his hand on my knee. I run my fingers along the back of that hand. I run them along his neck to his collarbone, slowly, like I've just fashioned him out of clay. I can't believe he's here. He touches the side of my thigh. I'm not looking at him, I'm just watching the various places where our skin meets. I am in a bit of a dream state. I didn't realize it until now, but while I have been getting myself together, I have also been waiting for this. On some level, I hoped that if I came back to myself, Wyatt would come back to me too. Sam I am, and vice versa.

He pulls me into a hug. "Sam, I—"

"Not yet," I say. We've done a lot of talking, and whatever it is he has to say isn't going to feel better than Wyatt's being right here next to me. I lie back on the futon and pull him down on top of me. His face hovers above mine, and he's taking me in. He sweeps the hair out of my eyes and runs his thumbs along my cheekbones. There's nearly no space between our lips, but I wait. I'm waiting for Wyatt to return to me, to *choose* this, choose us. He finally kisses me, and the warmth of his lips on mine sends a current through-out my body. It is still true—there are no two people who are more right together. There was a time when it felt like Wyatt and I could kiss for hours, when kissing him and feeling his chest pressed against mine was enough of a thrill. This is no longer the case, and I need to get out of my clothes. I pull off my shirt and then pull off his so that I can feel our skin together, like I am peeling off layers to get us back to our most natural state.

"Sam," he breathes into my shoulder. "Are you sure you want to do this?"

"Yes," I say.

"I really did have a thing I was going to tell you," he says into my neck. But he's breathless, and I don't know how we could possibly have a conversation anyway.

"Please," I say, and put my fingers on his lips to quiet him, just the way he put his fingers on mine so many years ago.

He kisses my fingers. "Okay." My legs remember exactly how to wrap themselves around his, and my senses are whispering about a time long past—he tastes the same, feels the same. But he's surer now, and so am I. The feel of his body tied up in mine makes me go completely liquid, as if I have dissolved into him. I do not remember that happening fourteen years ago.

"I TOTALLY PLANNED for this," I say. We're lying on the futon under my blanket, and I reach for a bottle of water I left on the table.

"Clearly you moved in here, desperately waiting for me." I rest my head on his chest, feeling the rumble of his chuckle, and he runs his fingers along my spine. I'm trying to remember if he used to do this, but it doesn't matter. None of this feels like it's for old times' sake. This is new.

"I waited a long time," I say. I don't know if I'm talking about the week I've been living on Long Island or my whole adult life.

"I'm an idiot," he says, and kisses my forehead.

"Agreed." I roll onto him and rest my chin on my hands. I can't stop smiling.

He moves a piece of my hair behind my ear. "So, I told Carlyle I wouldn't write any more songs for Missy, and now he's busy making sure no music producer ever wants to work with me again. Like, it took ten minutes for that film producer to call my manager and say they're going in another direction."

"Oh. I'm sorry." And I am. It breaks my heart to think that Wyatt's career could be taken from him. I kiss his neck and rest my head there. "So what does that mean? You're washed up? Staying here? It's working for me, you should try it. I have so much soup."

He laughs. "I'm self-employed, actually."

"Congratulations?" I don't know what this means.

"I'm going to start recording my own songs, myself. I don't know why I let Carlyle be the authority on whether people would like my voice. And they're my songs."

"I like your voice," I say, and sit up. I cover myself with the blanket, because I have the feeling I need to brace myself. "I really do. And I think everyone at the Owl Barn did too. They went nuts, right? Didn't they? It was kind of a weird night." The moon is lighting up the inside of the treehouse, and I can see Wyatt's face perfectly. I want to stop time.

"I'm writing a new album, and I dropped the first song last night. I just put it online. It's kind of a thing already. It's called *Summer Songs*. I don't need a music producer, as it turns out." Wyatt's hands are behind his head, and he's watching me take this in.

He's smiling, so I smile back. But I'm ashamed of myself. I was happier thirty seconds ago when I thought he'd blown it and was coming home. If he can make it on his own and people like his voice, I'm going to lose him again.

"Google me," he says.

I roll my eyes. "I get it, you're a big shot. I'm impressed."

"No. Seriously, google me."

I find my shorts on the floor, pull my phone out of my pocket, and type "Wyatt Pope." What appears makes no sense to me, because I thought it existed only in my mind. It's the drawing I did of Wyatt writing a song, complete with the hole in the top where the old nail pushed through. His eyes are looking directly at me, exactly how I remember that moment I was climbing up the ladder. Along the bottom are the words "Wyatt Pope Summer Songs."

I look up at Wyatt. "I don't understand."

"It's my album cover. I'm releasing songs as I have them. But that's the artwork. That's what I'm coming back to." He's smiling at me, and there is something I should say but I'm speechless. "You're not going to sue me, are you? It was a gift. I have witnesses."

"No. I mean, yes, it was a gift." And then, because I just have to get the words out of my head, "It's so good."

Wyatt laughs and takes my hands. "It really is. I've had it up every place I've ever lived." I lie back down next to him and hug him tight. I don't know why it matters now, but I'm glad he didn't completely leave me behind all those years ago. It's strange to think something has disintegrated and then find out it has not.

Wyatt notices I'm crying before I do. "Sam, what's going on? This is good news. I'm free."

I don't want to look at him. "God, I'm so selfish. That's great. Of course, it's great. But just a minute ago you were here and maybe staying and now you've got an album and you're going to leave and do a big thing."

"I'm going to stay and do a big thing." He takes my face in his hands and wipes a tear with his thumb. "I'm going to stay here and finish the album. You're going to help me."

I wipe my eyes on the blanket. "Oh."

"Sam, I got my voice back," he says. "I can do whatever I want."

"With me?"

"Want me to start from the beginning again?"

"No. I get it. I just . . ." I am equal parts afraid and happy. Having something like this to lose is more than I can fathom as I'm trying to start my life over again. I don't want to spend a few months in Wyatt's arms and then send him back to Los Angeles while I get reacquainted with Dr. Judy. I don't know if he's staying or if he's *staying*. "I love our friendship. It feels kind of risky to do this."

"I see no risk."

I don't say anything. I keep my head on his chest and concentrate on the way his skin touches mine down the whole length of my body. This is too much to lose.

Wyatt tilts my chin so that we're eye to eye. "I'm done writing songs about how much I loved you when we were kids. Missy can have those songs. My new album is about how I feel now. And when I'm done, I'm going to write another one about how a year's gone by and I'm even more in love with you." He's looking at me with such certainty and confidence that I can almost hear these songs. "After that I'll probably write songs about being married to a crazy art teacher. I love you, Sam. I've loved you my whole life. There's no risk."

"Oh." I'm in the most improbable situation, grown up and naked in this treehouse with Wyatt, who loves me. He's wrong, of course; there's a ton of risk in loving someone like this. But I know it's worth it, and for the first time in years, everything makes sense. "I love you too."

He kisses me for a long time. Just slowly, like it's not going anywhere. Like he's not going anywhere. "I should have done this years ago," he says.

"I think you did."

"No, I mean come here to see you. I think I needed to get backed into a corner."

"Who backed you into a corner?"

Wyatt looks away like he's embarrassed. And I can't imagine why, because we're both completely naked on a lot of levels. "I brought the music festival here because Michael told me you were getting married."

I am shocked and not shocked.

"I rented the house from my mom. I paid for the renovation at the Owl Barn. I just wanted to see you again, and make sure you were happy and with someone good. I thought I'd get closure."

And I like this. I like knowing that it wasn't some act of fate or the draw of a washed-up tennis player that brought Wyatt back here to me. He chose me and got on a plane. "I am happy, and I am with someone good," I say.

He pulls me close. "Great. This is actually just the closure I needed."

62

The weekend of my wedding that is not to be, my parents and Gracie come out to Long Island. My dad wants to check to see if the boiler is leaking the way it does almost every October. Or at least that's his cover; I think they want to spy on us. Granny and Gramps show up too, because they already wrote "Long Island" on their calendar in ink. Also, the spying.

"Hey-ho!" my dad booms on Friday evening when he comes through the door. "Are there squatters in my house?"

Wyatt's pulling glasses out of the dishwasher and, for a split second, looks like he's been caught doing something he shouldn't. He seems to remember himself and walks over to hug my dad. It's an actual hug, not a quickie, and when my dad pulls away he is a little misty.

"I'm just so happy," he says, putting his duffel bag on the table.

"Tell me about it," says Wyatt.

My mom comes in with a plastic bag full of used Metro-

Cards. I give her a hug and ask what they're for. "I'm not sure," she says. "God, you look beautiful." She touches my face the way she likes to, with both hands so she can take it in with multiple senses.

"Thanks. I'm just— It's so—" I'm not sure what I'm trying to say.

"Oh, I know, sweetie," she says.

Gracie lugs a suitcase through the front door and is not the person I remember. It's only been two months but she's maybe grown an inch, and her hair is in a loose single braid. Soon it will be completely down and she'll be using it to gesture. Maybe even toss. She's rounding that corner, and I'm not sure how I feel about it. I'm sorry for what she's leaving behind, that completely unselfconscious free-form reality of childhood. I have a strong urge to protect her, to shuttle her through these years quickly so she can be thirty. Or, better, forty. But that's not how caterpillars get there. It's not how any of us do.

"My friends are like freaking out about 'Summer Still,'" she tells Wyatt. "I mean it's so perfect for right now, like when it's getting colder?" She's picked up "like" and the up-talk at the end of a sentence. I want to know who's responsible for this.

"Thanks," says Wyatt. "Sam and I are hoping to have a whole album ready by the end of the winter." He puts his arm around me, and I notice they've all paused to observe this.

"Sam's helping?" my dad asks.

"Well, she helps by leaving for a lot of the day so I can work."

I give him a smile and nudge. "That's not true. He works all the time. I think he sleeps while I'm at the library."

"This is so weird," says Gracie. "I guess I'm the only one in the family that never saw you two madly in love."

"Gracie," my mom says. Though I don't know what she's admonishing her for. Apparently, neither does she, because she smiles. "Granny and Gramps will be here in a bit. We've got stuff to grill, if it's not too cold out there. Travis and Hugh are right behind us."

"TONIGHT WAS SUPPOSED to be your rehearsal dinner," Travis says because he's such a troublemaker. "Where was that going to be again?"

"That washed-up tennis player's park," I say.

"Weather would have been nice for it," says Granny, and my mom nods. Wyatt gives my shoulder a squeeze, as if I need to be reminded of how great it is that we are not currently at my rehearsal dinner.

"Well, let's consider this a rehearsal dinner," my dad says. "Because I'm still paying for dinner for fifty at the Old Sloop Inn tomorrow night. Never got our deposit back, so I just held the reservation to piss them off."

"I'm sorry, Dad," I say.

"It's no big deal," he says, and smiles at my mom.

"Just tell them," my mom says.

My dad puts his hands on the table and considers us for a few seconds before he speaks. "There's a lot of interest in my new series. I have a show at the Nufriti-Greene Gallery in December. It's called *Lifeline*."

"Oh, Dad!" Travis and I are on our feet to hug him. "This must feel so good."

"It's about damn time," says Gramps to his glass.

"It feels like if you were starving to death and found out you could create a cheeseburger with your own hands," my dad says, his eyes a little misty.

"What's the new series? Can we see it?" I ask.

"It's very simple actually. It came to me the night you left Jack and Gracie grabbed your hand at the table. There are no straight lines, just connections, hinges, where we reach for each other and pull each other up. People will say it looks like a bunch of gulls flying, but it's really people holding hands."

"Honestly," Gramps says, and we laugh.

Wyatt raises his glass. "To *Lifeline*." We drink to that.

My dad's quiet for a second. "But, seriously, if any of you people want to get married tomorrow, speak now."

I know he's kidding, but I look at Wyatt and think, *Yes, I want to marry him tomorrow.* But not there and not in such a rush. The dress I wanted to buy when I was marrying Jack is the dress I always imagined marrying Wyatt in. I'm going to see that through.

Hugh pipes up: "Me." He puts his wineglass down on the table and considers us all before he speaks again. "I want to get married tomorrow." He turns to Travis. "Would you do that?"

"Wait, are you trying to say 'Will you marry me'?"

Hugh takes his hand. "Yes, that's what I'm trying to say. I've been so anxious about a big event and all that noise. Can we just gather fifty people last-minute and get it done without all the pressure? Because of course I want to marry you."

My mother is crying and my dad is smiling. Gracie has her hand over her mouth, presumably to keep from blurting something out and ruining the moment.

"Yes," Travis says. "Let's get married tomorrow."

We all cheer, and my dad puts his hands up to stop us. "Free wedding tomorrow—going once. Going twice," he says with a smile to Wyatt.

"No thanks, we're good," he says, taking my hand. "I've always planned to marry Sam on the beach."

ACKNOWLEDGMENTS

Just to save my high school friends some time: this is a work of fiction. All characters depicted in this novel are made up. If I dated a guy with a guitar, you would have known about it.

A heart full of thanks to my agent, Marly Rusoff, who has believed in me from the very first day and has been a warm and fierce advocate for me and my work. My favorite of her heroic acts was introducing me to my editor, Tara Singh Carlson. Tara, thank you for your patience in coaxing this novel out of me and then shaping it into something that feels exactly right. What a gift it has been to be guided by your big brain and keen sense of story.

Thank you to my team at G. P. Putnam's Sons—Ashley Di Dio, Katie McKee, Nicole Biton, Ashley McClay, Alexis Welby, Molly Pieper, Emily Mileham, Maija Baldauf, Erin Byrne, Claire Winecoff, and the great Sally Kim. The kindness you have shown me and the effort you have put into getting my books out into the world have been staggering. Special thanks to the sales force for working so enthusiastically to get me on the shelves.

Thank you to the brilliant cover designer Sanny Chiu for taking such care to create covers that make my books pop off the shelves; and thank you to Aja Pollock, my whip-smart copy editor, whose understanding of grammar and how time works completely outshines my own. Thank you to Ashley Tucker, the interior designer who made my books such a lovely visual reading experience.

In the category of people who are there when I need them—I am so grateful to psychologist Brook Picotte, who vetted Dr. Judy and Sam's state of mind. Thank you to David Wilson, who talked hedges and surfing with me and never asked why. And to my sister, Stefanie Wilson, who took me in during a revision panic and made me snacks while I wrote in her attic. There really is nothing like a sister.

Thank you, always, to my writing friends for standing up and cheering me on. I am so happy to be working in a field where the better we all do, the better we all do.

The book world is full of so many bighearted and creative people, and I am so thankful for their kindness. Thank you to the independent booksellers, the librarians, the Instagrammers, the TikTokers, and the whole world of book reviewers for all you do to get books into readers' hands. Your work is surely paving the path to a better world.

To my sons, only one of whom has read this book (yes, cash changed hands), thank you for all the ways you have bent and grown around the recent downturn in household services. Thank you for asking about my work and encouraging me along the way. I am beyond proud of the young men you've become.

Tom. What can I say? If you played the guitar, someone else would have scooped you up a decade before I had the chance. So thank you for being the best part of my life and for not playing the guitar.

Same Time Next Summer

Annabel Monaghan

A Conversation with Annabel Monaghan

Discussion Questions

A Playlist

BOOK
ENDS

PUTNAM
—EST. 1838—

A Conversation
with Annabel Monaghan

What inspired you to write *Same Time Next Summer*?

The Philadelphia Story has always been one of my favorite movies. At the highest level, it's the story of Tracy Lord (Katharine Hepburn) who comes home to get married and finds her ex-husband C. K. Dexter Haven (Cary Grant) living next door. When I was a kid, I loved it for the funny dialogue and the scandalous way the adults were always making bad choices. When I was older, it made me think about how we move through heartbreak—both in our own relationships and within our families—and often reinvent ourselves to keep our hearts safe in the future.

I wanted to write a story that explores how heartbreak shapes identity. I find that when people are about nine years old, they know exactly who they are. But, of course, life happens. We grow, we rub up against the world, we get our hearts broken, and we might even be let down by the people we trust the most. And all of that friction shapes who we are as adults. I am fascinated by the lengths we go to in order to reframe our life stories and reimagine ourselves. Some people can do this for their whole lives and safely inhabit a new, false persona. But I think the truth usually surfaces, and the happiest people are living their most authentic lives.

In your debut novel, *Nora Goes Off Script,* the main characters fall in love later in life as adults. Why did you decide for the relationship in *Same Time Next Summer* to be about first love? What was your favorite part of writing this dynamic?

The great thing about first love is that we don't know enough to protect ourselves from it. We dive in heart-first, and it feels endless until it ends. In my memory, you don't even go looking for first love, it just sort of finds you and, once it gathers momentum, it feels inevitable. While I loved writing about adults later in life because of all of the complications Nora and Leo brought into their relationship, I also loved writing about first love because of its singularity of purpose. First love is a highly focused freight train of emotions, and I wanted to write about those very real feelings with the respect they deserve. Sometimes first love lasts, mostly it doesn't. But it informs how we approach love in the future.

Sam's family home on Long Island, New York, feels like the perfect oasis to escape to for the summer. Is this beach town based on a real place?

Oak Shore is a made-up Long Island town. Long Island felt like a perfect place to set this story because of its natural beauty and its proximity to Manhattan. When I think of Long Island in the summer, I think of hydrangea growing like weeds and the dunes moving with the breeze on the beach. I imagined a lot of sensory memories being stored on those beaches, and it felt like a good place to fall in love.

When we return to where our childhoods happened, it's hard not to slip back in time. I grew up in Los Angeles and went to the beach most days. The ocean was not right outside my door—I drove there—but the anticipation that I felt driving to the beach became part of the experience. Sam walks through the dunes that give way to the sand and the ocean in the same way I drove down the California Incline onto the Pacific Coast Highway. There is so much sensory memory tied up in this for me. When I am at that beach, the smell of the air and the rough feel of dried salt on my skin whispers at me about who I used to be.

Music plays an important role in Sam and Wyatt's love story. Do you have a connection to music or the arts, and why did you choose to include this aspect in *Same Time Next Summer*?

I love music as a listener (and as an awkward but enthusiastic dancer), but I have no talent for it and don't play an instrument. But still, I find that certain songs contain full years of my life, and others can take me back to a single moment. This is particularly true of summer music: songs that played over and over on the radio on long, lazy days can bring back the smell of Coppertone and the feel of hot sand under my feet. There are studies that show that the music we listened to during our teenage years actually attaches itself to our emotional memory in a much deeper way than music we hear for the first time as adults. If anything was going to unlock the fortress around Sam's heart, it would be music.

Who was your favorite character to write, and why?

Probably Wyatt. He's a bit introverted like I am, and I liked watching him bide his time with Sam, both as a kid and as an adult. He keeps his feelings hidden for a lot of the novel, but I could always tell where he was emotionally. Also, it was fun writing about a person with a secret, who isn't exactly lying but isn't exactly being forthcoming either.

Why did you decide to structure the novel between the past and present, and from Sam and Wyatt's perspectives in the past? How do you think this storytelling technique adds to the reading experience?

Memory is such a subjective thing. If I told you the story of an old summer romance of mine, I'd give you the general idea of when it was and where we were, but I wouldn't do it justice because I can't quite see the details from this far away. I might tell you that I really liked him, but I would trivialize the whole thing because I don't remember exactly the way it felt when he looked at me or what it was like when we broke up. This is especially true for this story because of how much work Sam has done to dismiss the importance of her relationship with Wyatt. I thought it was important for the reader to experience what falling in love was like for Sam and Wyatt in real time so they could understand why it still mattered.

Although this is a story about Sam and Wyatt, *Same Time Next Summer* also feels like a story of the complicated nature of family. Why is it important

that family be represented in this story? How does it inform Sam and Wyatt's choices and behaviors?

I grew up in a family and I'm now raising one, and I can tell you one thing for sure: a family is a complex living organism. Everything that happens to any family member affects the others. Our moods, our victories, and our horrible mistakes shape how everyone else in the family grows. We are limited by one another's beliefs and thrust forward by one another's successes. This is why family stories intrigue me so much. Human beings who are woven together by proximity, genetics, and love have a lot to sort out.

Without giving anything away, did you always know how the story would end?

No. I never do. I knew tonally how it was going to end, but I did not know how I'd get there. But once I got to know Wyatt a little better and saw where he was a tiny bit wounded, I knew what he had to do to find his voice.

What do you want readers to take away from *Same Time Next Summer*?

We are all great survivors, and we have endless ways that we adapt to protect ourselves. There's a balance between being safe and truly living, and it's our job to determine how much risk our hearts can take and how deeply we are willing to love. This is a story about returning to your truest, bravest self. And it's an exploration of whether the safety that comes with loving someone at arm's length is worth giving up the joy of loving someone with your whole heart.

What's next for you?

I'm writing a love story that involves a skate boarder who is pretending to be a divorce attorney. And, no, I don't know how it's going to end.

Discussion Questions

1. Did you and your family have a place you would visit for the summer when you were growing up? Or possibly a special vacation you went on? What was your fondest memory from that time?

2. Who was your first love? How much of an impact did that relationship have on your life, and what did you learn from it?

3. Compare and contrast the feelings Sam has for Wyatt and Jack. Why is Sam drawn to each of them? What do you think is the most important quality a romantic relationship should have?

4. Is there a song that makes you think about your first love, or another relationship? Why?

5. What was your favorite scene, and why?

6. When you are stressed or need to clear your head, what activity do you turn to and why?

7. When Sam and Wyatt are teenagers, they each reflect on how different their families are from one another. How do you think their family dynamics shaped who they each became?

8. Were you surprised to learn the truth behind Sam and Wyatt's breakup? If you were in their shoes, how would you have reacted?

9. If Sam hadn't gone to therapy, do you think she would have gone down a different path in life?

10. What are your thoughts about the ending?

A Playlist

I don't listen to music while I write because I find it very distracting. I can't seem to concentrate on the words in my head when there are other words spinning around the room. But when I'm not writing, I am walking and listening to music and thinking about my story. There are a handful of songs that always took me to the beach or that felt like something Wyatt might write. And, yes, you'll find the selection a bit eclectic—who, besides me, remembers Little River Band?

Songs that felt like Wyatt:

"Iris" by Goo Goo Dolls
"A Murder of One" by Counting Crows
"Take It Easy on Me" by Little River Band
"Hold You in My Arms" by Ray LaMontagne
"Wild Horses" by The Rolling Stones
"Thinking Out Loud" by Ed Sheeran
"Yellow" by Coldplay

Songs that took me to the beach:

"Watermelon Sugar" by Harry Styles

"Sunshine on My Shoulders" by John Denver

"Wouldn't It Be Nice" by The Beach Boys

Songs to make Sam cry:

"Who Knew" by Pink

"Wrecking Ball" by Miley Cyrus

"1 Step Forward, 3 Steps Back" by Olivia Rodrigo

"So Far Away" by Carole King

"Romeo and Juliet" by Dire Straits

"Stay" by Rihanna

"Sam, I Am" by Missy McGee

ABOUT THE AUTHOR

© Jo Bryan Photography

Annabel Monaghan is the author of Indie Next and LibraryReads pick *Nora Goes Off Script*, as well as two young adult novels and *Does This Volvo Make My Butt Look Big?*, a selection of laugh-out-loud columns that appeared in *The Huffington Post, The Week*, and *The Rye Record*. She lives in Rye, New York, with her family.